SINKING SHIP

Frank and Joe made their way toward the front of the half-sunken freighter, trying to keep their balance as the ship rocked back and forth.

"One, two, three!" Frank chanted as the brothers threw their combined strength into opening the heavy steel door of the cargo hold. "The fire must have warped the metal," Frank remarked as they staggered into the dark room. They stood gazing at the charred wreckage.

"Wow," Joe said. "Must have been some fire."

Before Frank could answer, a large wave hit the ship. The boys were pitched forward. As they struggled to their knees, they heard the metal door clang shut. The hold was plunged into total darkness. Joe felt for the door, then tried to pull it open.

"Frank!" Joe shouted, fighting the panic that rose in his chest. "The door's jammed. We're trapped inside!"

Books in THE HARDY BOYS CASEFILES® Series

Available from ARCHWAY Paperbacks

LETHAL CARGO

FRANKLIN W. DIXON

AN ARCHWAY PAPERBACK
Published by POCKET BOOKS

New York   London   Toronto   Sydney   Tokyo   Singapore

AN ARCHWAY PAPERBACK *Original*

An Archway Paperback published by
POCKET BOOKS, a division of Simon & Schuster Inc.
1230 Avenue of the Americas, New York, NY 10020

Copyright © 1992 by Simon & Schuster Inc.
Produced by Mega-Books of New York, Inc.

ISBN: 0-671-73103-3

First Archway Paperback printing September 1992

10 9 8 7 6 5 4 3 2 1

THE HARDY BOYS, AN ARCHWAY PAPERBACK and colophon are registered trademarks of Simon & Schuster Inc.

THE HARDY BOYS CASEFILES is a trademark of Simon & Schuster Inc.

Cover art by Brian Kotzky

Printed in the U.S.A.

IL 6+

Chapter

1

"FORGET BEING A DETECTIVE!" Joe Hardy called back to his brother, Frank. He shifted the air pillow under his head. *"This* is the life I was meant to lead!"

Frank laughed at Joe from the cockpit of the *Sun Dancer.* While the dark-haired eighteen-year-old steered the forty-foot yacht across the choppy Caribbean Sea from the area behind the mast, Joe lay stretched out on a blanket on deck, soaking up some rays. Joe's blond hair had gotten even lighter the past week, and his new tan contrasted sharply with his neon green swim trunks and purple-mirrored shades.

"You're a little young to retire, aren't you?" Frank asked him with a grin.

"What?" Joe sat up and cupped a hand to his

ear. "I can't hear you over the noise of the flapping sails."

"Okay, so they're luffing a little." Frank realigned the mainsail. "I'm having a hard time telling where the wind's coming from."

"No problem." Joe lay back down, gazing up at the cloudless sky. "After a free week in the sun, I'm not about to complain."

Frank leaned back against the padded pilot's seat. The two brothers were sailing the single-masted sloop *Sun Dancer* from the Caribbean island of Saint Martin to Fort Lauderdale, Florida. Henry Stefano, the sloop's owner and an old friend of their father, had offered the boys a free week on Saint Martin in exchange for transporting his yacht from the island to his beach house in Florida. So far, Frank reflected, it had been a no-lose deal; sailing the luxurious *Sun Dancer* was more a bonus than a chore.

"It might not be this easy all the way, Joe," Frank warned his brother. "According to the ship-to-shore radio, a tropical storm is headed this way. We'll have to detour to Puerto Rico to wait it out."

"A storm?" Joe sat up again and took off his sunglasses, revealing the excitement in his blue eyes. "When's it due?"

"Not till tomorrow afternoon, so calm down," Frank answered with a chuckle. "We'll be able to make San Juan, Puerto Rico, by morning, even if I am sailing this beauty more or less alone."

"Hey, I took the morning shift, remember?"

"Right—half of which we spent eating breakfast, and the other half diving off the boat," Frank reminded him. He sighed. "Speaking of diving, how about another swim break right about now? These gusts are no fun to fight, and I'm burning up in this sun."

"Well . . ." Joe swiveled to the right and left. "If you're sure we won't get ambushed by Hurricane Godzilla out here in the middle of nowhere—"

"What a wimp!" Frank tossed an air pillow at his brother.

"Man overboard!" Laughing, Joe pretended that the pillow had knocked him over, and he fell backward into the restless turquoise sea.

Because the wind was so gusty, the boys took turns swimming while the other remained on board to control the boat and make sure the line with the life preserver trailed in the water near the swimmer. First Joe, then Frank dove under the choppy waves, using snorkel gear to chase fish and look for giant sea turtles. Overhead, several sea gulls hovered, hoping for handouts. Except for the birds, the entire world seemed empty of everyone but the Hardys.

After their swim, Frank grilled hamburgers for lunch in the galley. Then Joe, plotting their altered course on the boat's nautical maps, took his turn as skipper while Frank napped in the large cabin below. When Frank took over again after dinner, he saw that they were on course for Puerto Rico.

"Not bad sailing, Joe," Frank admitted as he relieved his brother. "If I ever get the chance to enter the America's Cup race, you're my choice for first mate."

"Thanks, boss," Joe said sarcastically. "I guess that means I get to turn in."

While Joe slept, Frank skippered, trimming the sails against the increasingly strong winds and enjoying the silence of the dark night. Most of the stars were now hidden by dark, fast-moving clouds, but a full moon still cast a single wedge of light across the waves. After a few hours Frank spotted a tiny island in his path. Idly, he steered toward it.

"Wake up, Joe. It's your turn at the helm," Frank called, gracefully tacking the yacht toward the lee, or protected, side of the steep, rocky point of land. It was completely deserted, at least what he could see of it.

Joe appeared from belowdecks in a pair of khaki shorts, yawning and scratching his football-hardened belly. "What time is it?" he mumbled.

"Two-thirty." Frank kept his eyes on the island. Close to shore, he was now sailing parallel to the coast and back out to the open sea.

"How can you see your watch? It's pitch-black out here."

"The moon's been going in and out of the clouds." Frank readjusted the sails, which were once again luffing. "Okay. She's all yours. Wake me up in—"

He stopped in midsentence, listening to a noise coming from the far side of the island. "What's that?" he asked.

"It sounds like an engine." Joe peered at the rocky shore as their boat skimmed swiftly past it. "It's really loud, though. Maybe it's a—"

"Shhh!" Frank said. "I think it's—" He moved quickly to the left rail, the port side. "Oh, wow!"

The moon, moving out from behind a cloud, shone down on an enormous black shape moving parallel to the *Sun Dancer* on the other side of the island hills. Silhouetted against the darkness, blacker than the dark night, was a huge cargo ship, as high as a four-story building and longer than a city block.

"Come about!" Frank yelled. "Joe, the wheel!"

The roar of the ship's engine rang in Frank's ears as Joe frantically tried to avoid a collision. The sloop turned sharply, forcing Frank against the rail. "Not so hard!" he shouted to his brother. "We'll turn over!"

As the *Sun Dancer* cleared the island, Frank saw a series of high waves radiating toward them from the bow of the darkened ship. "Watch out—" he called to Joe, but it was too late. The first of the waves reached the sailboat and sent it flying.

"Whoa!" Frank shouted as the sloop rode the wave sideways high into the air, half-turned, then plunged down into the trough on the other side. It moved directly toward the hulking shape. Water whooshed over the deck, slamming Frank against the wheel.

Twisting in the surging water, Frank grasped the base of the wheel and hung on. As the wave pulled against his torso, he checked frantically for Joe.

"I'm here, Frank!" Joe clung to the seat, staggering to keep his balance on the listing boat. The noise from the cargo ship's engine drowned out his voice as the waves sent the *Sun Dancer* straight for the freighter's side. There were no running lights on board, and Frank saw that trying to get the crew's attention would be useless. The *Sun Dancer* was moving too quickly, and besides, Frank could see no one on the ship's deck.

"Hold on, Joe." Frank shouted to be heard above the roar of the cargo ship's engines. "We're going to crash!"

Frank and his brother held on as the ship's massive hull rumbled through the waves. Just as the *Sun Dancer* was slipping the last few yards toward a sure crash with the stern, the freighter sped up and moved out of the sailboat's path.

The sloop slipped directly behind the huge ship, unharmed.

Weak with relief, Frank turned to his brother. "That was close!" he shouted. "What *was* that, anyway?"

"Watch out, Frank!" Joe yelled. He was too late. Another deadly wave hit the sloop, throwing Frank halfway down the steps to the cabin. He smashed his head against the hatchway.

As the yacht fell into the trough of the wave, water washed over the deck, almost drowning Frank before it receded again. He forced his way up the steps, spluttering.

"Thanks for the warning," Frank gasped as he reached the pilot's seat. He looked for his brother. No one was there.

"Joe!" Frank peered over the topside into the churning water. For an instant he thought he glimpsed a hand waving in the moonlight.

"Hold on!" Frank shouted. He looked around desperately. The line with the life preserver lay coiled next to the pilot's seat. Frank tossed the preserver toward the spot where he thought he'd seen the hand. A moment later he could make out Joe clinging to the ring float.

"And I thought *you* were the goner!" Joe gasped as Frank pulled him up onto the watery deck. "Thanks. I was sure I'd bought it that time."

"No problem, little brother." Frank collapsed beside his brother. "You'd do the same for me."

"Whoever's in charge of that ship has some major explaining to do," Joe said. "No running lights. No one on deck. And they obviously don't know sail has the right of way."

"And they're going to explain," Frank agreed, as angry as he'd ever been. "Let's sail."

Frank and Joe followed the ship, barely able to make out its shape in the darkness but able to track it well enough by ear. The wind picked up as dawn drew near. Both the ship and the sailboat would be better off in a safe harbor when the storm hit.

By daybreak the *Sun Dancer* was only half a mile behind the enormous ship. By the light of the rising sun, Frank inspected their unwitting attacker from the night before. "It's a wreck!" he said to Joe, taking in the rusty hull and general neglected appearance of the craft. "And listen. The engines have stopped." Joe maneuvered the sailboat closer, and the boys spotted the ship's name painted on the stern.

"S.S. *Laura Baines*," Joe read aloud.

"Look how low she's sitting in the water," Frank said. "There's no one on deck. And her lifeboats are gone. Those are the davit lines that should hold them on deck, hanging off the sides."

"You think she's been abandoned?" Joe asked.

"I don't see any other explanation. It looks

like it's just drifting now. I wonder what's going on?"

"We'd better put in a call to the coast guard." Joe reached for the radio's microphone. "We should be able to raise Puerto Rico."

Frank nodded, taking over at the wheel and moving the *Sun Dancer* closer to the old freighter. "Rats!" he heard Joe say. "We're out of range. Are you sure you know where we are?"

"Not positive," Frank replied, keeping his eyes on the mysterious ship as the wind whipped his dark hair off his face. "I assumed the freighter was making for Puerto Rico."

Frank peered up at the gathering clouds. "Time to forget about the ship and worry about getting out of here now," he said. "I have a feeling we can make it to Puerto Rico still, but first we have to figure out where we are exactly."

"What if we can't make it?" Joe demanded. "No one will know where to look for us. I can't believe you'd just follow that ship and get us off course like this."

"I do have a good idea where we are, and we can figure it out pretty quick. That ship ought to have a stronger radio than ours," he suggested. "If we can board her, we can contact the coast guard."

"Maybe there's someone still on board," Joe said.

He disappeared belowdecks to reappear with

9

a small battery-operated megaphone. He switched it on and shouted to the nearby ship, "Ahoy! Anyone aboard?"

There was no reply besides the lapping of the waves.

"I'll take a chance and board her and see what's going on," Joe decided. "I don't want to head off for Puerto Rico until someone knows we're here."

"Okay," Frank agreed uncertainly, steering the yacht toward the big ship. "I just hope we don't get arrested for illegally boarding her and that we don't scrape up Mr. Stefano's favorite toy."

Frank lowered the sloop's sails and started the small engine that would power them to the freighter. Fighting the choppy waves, Frank got to within a few feet of the *Laura Baines*. Joe, in the shorts and Hawaiian shirt he'd changed into after his dunking the night before, stood poised on the edge of the deck, waiting to make a leap for one of the davit lines.

"Here goes," Joe said, grabbing hold of a line. He pulled himself up on the rope, bracing his sneakered feet against the hull of the freighter.

"Careful!" Frank called, watching his brother as he held the sloop as steady as possible alongside the ship. The swell of the ocean was increasing noticeably, tossing the sloop about and even starting the freighter rolling. Frank saw his brother's feet slip and lose contact with the hull.

"Joe!" Frank yelled, watching his brother swing out from the ship on a davit line thirty feet above the water. Then he began swinging back toward the rusty hull. Joe had no choice but to hang on, Frank decided.

As Frank watched in horror, his brother was slammed against the iron ship, then pushed out again.

"Hold on, Joe!" Frank checked for another davit line. Maybe he could climb up and help his brother down.

Frank was too late. Thirty feet above him Joe lost his grip. He started falling, straight for the deck of the *Sun Dancer!*

Chapter

2

"HEEEELLP!" Joe yelled as he fell along the ship's curved side, clawing to regain hold of the rope. Below, the *Sun Dancer* zoomed up toward him. Joe continued to grope for the rope, but waited for the inevitable impact. Then, miraculously, his fingers closed around the rope.

Joe slid several yards before stopping himself mere feet above the deck of the bobbing sloop.

"Gee, Joe," he heard Frank say shakily. "How many heart attacks do you want to give me on this trip?"

"Just testing your reactions." Joe tried to ignore his trembling arm muscles as he hung on tightly. His palms burned, and he longed to plunge them into cool seawater, but knew the salt would make them feel worse. Instead, taking a deep breath and gritting his teeth, he started shimmying up the rope again.

"Hey!" he heard Frank yell. "Where do you think you're going?"

"To find that radio!" Joe yelled down at him. "That's what I was supposed to do, isn't it?"

"You're supposed to get right back down here before you get yourself killed! The waves aren't getting any lower!"

Frank's voice sounded fainter as Joe neared the deck of the freighter. Just when he felt he couldn't hang on any longer, he tumbled over the railing and collapsed onto the deck. The ship was heaving regularly in the ocean swells. A cool breeze struck Joe's face as he pulled himself to his feet. He recognized it as the first sure sign of a coming storm. After a quick wave down to Frank to show he was okay, he began to inspect the ship.

Cautiously, Joe climbed a set of narrow metal steps, called a companionway, to the ship's bridge, looking to the left and right as he moved. No one appeared on deck, and when Joe entered the bridge he saw that it, too, was deserted.

Feeling uneasy, Joe descended to the crew's quarters—but they, too, were empty. The rooms were a mess of scattered clothes. Joe guessed they had left in a hurry.

He headed back upstairs, found the radio room, and entered it, switching on the light inside. "Wow." He stared in disbelief around the room. "This is bizarre." The radio and radar and sonar equipment—the entire control panel, in fact—had been smashed to bits. A fire ax lay on the floor. Obviously, it had been used to do the dirty work. But why? Joe wondered. Who would want to tear up an old ship?

There was no point in staying on board. The ship must have been abandoned for a good reason, and Joe decided to get off, too.

As he passed the companionway down to the engine room, Joe heard a noise. He paused, listening.

There it was again. It sounded like a faint moaning. Somebody's down there! Joe realized. He raced down the metal ladder, then another and another, until he reached a catwalk above the engine room in the bowels of the ship. It was an enormous, hot metal-lined cavern full of thick hissing pipes and housing, and at its base he could see the ship's slowly revolving propeller shaft. Looking around, Joe spotted a large man staggering toward him on the metal catwalk lining the room.

It's the captain! Joe said to himself, recognizing the man's uniform.

Muttering incoherently, the master of the ship tottered toward Joe. At last he noticed Joe, and his eyes opened wide. "Get off my ship!" he roared. "She's mine, and you can't take her away!"

"I don't want to," Joe replied uncertainly,

backing away. "I just wanted to use your radio—"

"Ha!" The man staggered toward Joe and glared down at him. Joe Hardy was six feet tall, but the captain was taller. "You can't fool me. You're one of them!" he roared. Joe forced himself to remain where he was and stared levelly at the other man's sweat- and dirt-stained face with the bushy black brows.

The captain calmed down a little as he said uncertainly, "I *don't* know you, do I?" Then he started exploding again. "You must be with the commission, then—"

"No, sir, I—"

"Get off my ship!" The captain grabbed Joe by the shoulders and shoved him toward the ladder.

Joe clamped his sore hands on the captain's powerful wrists to keep himself from being knocked over. "Why don't you come with me, sir?" he asked, trying to stay calm. "My brother's waiting on our boat. We'll take you back to port. You can tell the authorities what happened, and—"

"I'm not going anywhere!" the captain bellowed, breaking free. "And you can't make me! I'm going down with my ship. I'm not giving you people an excuse to take away my license again!"

What's wrong with this guy? Joe wondered briefly. What license? Then he said calmly to the captain, "You've got me all wrong, sir. I'm not—"

"Get off!" The now-crazed captain flew at Joe's throat. Forced to defend himself, Joe aimed a well-directed blow at the captain's heavy jaw. The master of the *Laura Baines* went down in a heap.

"Sorry about that, sir," Joe said uneasily. He turned and ran up the ladder to get help.

On deck, Joe leaned over the rail and spotted Frank far below, trying to keep the *Sun Dancer* from knocking against the freighter. "Frank!" Joe called down to his brother. "I found the captain on board! I need help getting him off the ship!"

"I can't get her close enough—" Frank yelled back. "The waves—"

Joe thought quickly. He could see that Frank would risk smashing the *Sun Dancer* if he tried to get them off the *Laura Baines*. Joe and the captain could jump overboard into the water, but even if they didn't hurt themselves, Frank might not be able to pick them up in the rough seas.

"Frank!" Joe shouted. "Go to San Juan! Get help! We'll try to follow!"

Frank seemed to understand, though his reply was lost in the wind. He waved to Joe, made the "okay" sign, and turned away. In moments the yacht was sailing before the wind. Joe hurried back to the captain, who was just coming to.

"Are you all right, sir?" he asked, helping the large man to a sitting position.

"I—I think so," he said, rubbing his chin. "Somebody hit me."

"Uh, yeah. I guess that was me. You were— well, you must've thought I was someone else."

"Oh—right." The captain leaned back to scrutinize Joe. "Who are you, anyway? And how did you board my ship?"

"Joe Hardy, sir," Joe replied, sticking out his hand to shake the captain's. "My brother and I are sailing a friend's sloop to Florida. You nearly ran us over last night, and I boarded your ship to use your radio."

The captain grunted, shaking his head. "I'm not surprised you were almost run down. Who knows who was steering the *Laura Baines* then."

Joe stared at him. "Weren't you?"

The captain shook his head, mopping his forehead with a huge handkerchief. "They locked me up and then abandoned ship," he said. "But first they tried to sink my ship, and me with her."

The ship swayed sharply with the force of a wave. "Storm's up," the captain said. "We'd better get her back under power. Follow me."

Joe sighed. *Who* locked the captain up, he wondered? His own crew? Joe didn't know there were mutinies anymore on ships like the *Laura Baines*.

The captain headed down into the engine

17

room. It was already at least a hundred degrees on the catwalk. Joe knew that the deeper they descended, the hotter it would be.

"When water isn't fed into the boiler, she shuts off automatically," the captain shouted as he crossed to the boiler.

"That'll get her going again," he said as the sound of rushing water filled the air. "In half an hour we'll cut off the inflow of water."

Turning to Joe, he smiled for the first time and rested a heavy hand on his shoulder. "By the way, I'm Captain Daniel Evans. Now, what do you say we go up to the bridge and take this boat to harbor?"

"Yes, sir!" Joe was relieved at the idea of escaping the engine room's extreme heat. He wondered how far Frank and the *Sun Dancer* were from Puerto Rico.

Joe followed the burly captain to the bridge as the engine sputtered into action, rumbling beneath their feet. There, Joe watched while Evans took the helm. "I'm better now," he said as he guided the ship through the heaving waves. It had begun to rain, but Joe noted that the seasoned sailor wasn't bothered by the storm.

"We were on a run from Manila to San Juan via the Panama Canal," the captain said abruptly as he manipulated the wheel. "Last night, a fire broke out in the fore cargo compartment—Number Three. I ordered the crew to fight the fire. They took so long that the flames got out of control. Then the mate came up, shouting that the rear cargo holds were flooding and for everyone to abandon ship.

"Well, that did it." The captain scowled at the tilting horizon. "I'm the one who gives orders on my ship! That's when one of them grabbed me from behind. They locked me in Number Four!"

"Who grabbed you?" Joe asked, fascinated. "Did you get a look at him?"

"It doesn't matter," the captain growled. "They were all in on it. The fire, the flood, everything. It was mutiny! Scheming, ungrateful—"

Joe broke in impatiently, "What happened next?"

The captain looked surprised. "I broke out, of course. Good thing a cargo compartment's not built like a brig. By that time the entire crew had abandoned ship. Luckily, I was able to put out the fire. I'd just finished when you turned up."

"But, Captain," Joe said, "if what you say is true, why did the crew leave? Isn't the point of a mutiny for the crew to take over the ship?"

"Point of the—what?" The captain turned a furious gaze on Joe. "You think I made this up?"

"N-no!" Joe was quick to say.

"It was a mutiny, all right, and they'll all be tried in maritime court as soon as I get my hands on them," the captain roared, red-faced under

19

the dirt and soot. "They tried to murder me—locked me up on a burning ship! I'll see they lose their seamen's cards, every one of them!"

"Right," said Joe, backing toward the door. Clearly the captain didn't want to hear about Joe's doubts. "What about those flooded cargo holds?"

"The doors are watertight," the captain said, turning back toward the horizon. "As long as the engine room stays dry, we can guide her into port, storm or no storm."

Joe coughed. "I have some bad news, Captain. Your communications room—it's been sabotaged."

"I know that, son," the captain said grimly, his focus dead ahead. "Don't you worry—I can guide this ship on instinct. Now, run down and turn off that water intake valve. The tank should be full by now."

Relieved to get away, Joe left the bridge, trying to work out Evans's story as he descended. Maybe Captain Evans was too angry to think straight about what had happened, but Joe knew the captain's version of events didn't make a lot of sense.

When Joe reached the bank of controls near the boiler, he turned the knob that controlled the intake pipe. He heard the rush of water slow down.

Suddenly the ship gave another lurch, and Joe knew she'd slammed into a huge wave. As he struggled to regain his balance, Joe heard the sickening sound of metal fracturing and of steel bolts pinging into oblivion as they shattered from stress.

"W-what?" Joe stammered, looking around wildly. To his right, a blast of water rushed into the room from the wall behind the boiler.

Joe scrambled up the stairs, sealing the hatch behind him before he climbed back up to the bridge.

"She's breaking up!" he yelled to the captain as he burst into the room. "The engine room's flooding fast!"

Even as the captain turned to stare at him, Joe felt the ship begin to list.

A sickening feeling overcame him. There were no lifeboats—no escape.

Chapter

3

FRANK WAS TOO BUSY struggling against the twenty-foot waves that threatened to swamp the *Sun Dancer* to worry about Joe. He had been sailing for about an hour and decided to try radioing the coast guard station at San Juan, Puerto Rico, again.

"Mayday! Mayday!" Frank shouted into the microphone as the boat flew up the side of an enormous wave, then slid sickeningly down onto the other side. "*Sun Dancer,* forty-foot sloop with one man aboard, caught in the storm. Others are stranded, too! We need help!"

Frank switched off the microphone.

"Read you. . . ." A woman's voice pierced the static. Eagerly, Frank leaned forward and fine-tuned the frequency.

"San Juan Coast Guard . . ." The voice faded in and out. "Give us your coordinates. Over."

Pouncing on his charts, Frank read his coordinates loud and clear. Then he waited for a reply. This time, the voice seemed clearer.

"We read you, *Sun Dancer*," it said. "This is Lieutenant Brown of the San Juan Coast Guard. Turn north fourteen degrees. You should be in the clear in fifteen minutes. Over."

"Roger, Lieutenant! I read you. Have you heard from the freighter *Laura Baines*? Over!" Frank shouted.

"*Sun Dancer*, we show no *Laura Baines* in the area. We will be on the lookout. Over."

Worried, Frank forced himself to concentrate on guiding the sailboat through the storm. "Fifteen minutes," he muttered as rain began pelting down, soaking him. "You can make it, boat. And, Joe, you'd better make it, too."

Joe stood watching Captain Evans peer through the driving rain. "I told him she ought to be scrapped," Joe heard him growl. "But no. 'One more voyage,' he tells me. Crazy fool—"

"Captain!" Joe moved forward and grabbed Evans's arm. "Didn't you hear me? The ship is going down!"

"Don't worry, kid. You're sailing with Captain Daniel Evans. I'll bring us in, don't you worry."

Suddenly the older man's face lit up. He gave

23

Joe a hearty slap on the back. "I know this place! We're saved, kid!"

Joe peered through the window. All he could see were waves crashing against a jagged reef. "Are you kidding?" Joe shouted. "This is a reef. We'll be torn to pieces!" Joe turned and started out. If Captain Evans was crazy enough to steer them into the reef, Joe was going to inflate a raft right now.

"Come back here, son," the captain roared after him. "Look to the far side of the reef—the leeward side!"

Joe stopped. At the far end of the reef, the waves were calmer, their force broken by the nearer reef barriers.

"I can guide her in there," the captain assured him. "We're practically in shouting distance of San Juan. Those lily-livered men of mine better watch out for their hides now! I'll get them the minute we hit land!"

If the engine holds long enough, Joe thought grimly. As Joe watched, the reef slid not fifty yards past the limping *Laura Baines*.

At last they cleared the reef, and the captain swung the enormous, lopsided craft about in the suddenly clear waters of the leeward side. With the ship pointed into the wind, the captain gunned the engine to send her onto the beach.

"See, son," he bragged, "this reef has been a graveyard for many a sailor, but it can be a friend if you know how to use it."

Suddenly there was a soft thump. Joe and the captain were thrown forward against the window of the bridge. The ship had stopped cold.

"Ha! What did I tell you?" the captain shouted, clapping Joe on the back. "Safely beached! You're sailing with the best, young fella. Daniel Evans, best cargo hauler in the Caribbean! Ha, ha, ha!"

Joe shook his head, laughing. Captain Evans was one of the craziest guys he had run into in a long time, but the man sure knew what he was doing.

Just as Lieutenant Brown had promised Frank, the rain and wind began to subside after fifteen minutes of sailing. The waves remained high, but the sky ahead was cloudless.

Frank was ecstatic as he rounded the breakwater and saw colorful San Juan harbor. Pink-and blue-painted old-fashioned buildings squatted in front of modern towering ones. The waterfront resembled every other waterfront around the world, though—grimy piers, heavy cranes, and long, low warehouses huddled close to the water. Huge freighters lay at anchor, waiting to discharge their cargo.

"You'll see the marina in a minute, on the lee shore," the radio voice told Frank. "After you're tied up, please stop by to give us more details on your brother's whereabouts. We've

25

learned that the *Laura Baines* was in our area, so any help would be appreciated. Over."

"Will do, Lieutenant," Frank said.

Frank turned his attention to easing the *Sun Dancer* into San Juan's attractive Club Nautico Marina. This section of the docks was definitely more appealing than the cargo area, he noted. The handsome piers were clean and sanded, the slips were filled with luxury yachts of all sizes, and on the shore a large café sported flags from around the world. Looking at it, it was hard for Frank to remember that his brother was still waiting to be rescued.

After checking in with the harbormaster, Frank hurried along the marina's boardwalk to the coast guard station. On the way, the smell of good food from the restaurant at the Club Nautico Café reminded him that it was way past lunchtime. Food would have to wait until Joe was safe, though.

Behind a chest-high counter in the coast guard's reception area, an officer stood turned away, working while a ship-to-shore radio spouted static and conversation. The wall above the radio was covered with charts and wall-mounted equipment.

"Excuse me, sir?" Frank said to the officer.

When the officer turned to face him, Frank saw she was female. Smiling, she took off her cap, revealing short blond hair, a pretty, freckled face, and startlingly green eyes. "Hi, there," she said, offering her hand across the counter. "I can tell by your bewildered expression that you must be the skipper of the *Sun Dancer*. I'm Lieutenant Lily Jean Brown."

"You're Lieutenant B-Brown?" Frank stammered, stepping back. "Wow! I mean—sorry, I guess I just didn't expect you to be so—"

"So young?" the lieutenant said. "It just seems that way because you aged about five years in the past hour."

"The ride in was so exciting I forgot what I must look like," Frank admitted, checking out his soggy T-shirt, shorts, ruined deck shoes.

"It's okay. The coast guard's required to rescue any sailor, no matter how bad he looks," the lieutenant teased. "Come on back here. I want you to show me where you last saw the *Laura Baines*."

Frank and the lieutenant bent over the charts and plotted the ship's position together. Frank couldn't help noticing that Lieutenant Brown looked as cute as her voice had sounded sensible on the radio. He liked the way her hair smelled—fresh and clean. The image of Callie Shaw, his girlfriend back in Bayport, appeared in Frank's mind, and he moved his nose away from the lieutenant's hair.

"Looking good," Lieutenant Brown said as she scribbled notes on a yellow pad. "We'll send a plane out to locate them first thing tomorrow."

27

"Tomorrow! Why not now?" Frank asked anxiously.

"Two reasons—the weather's too heavy over the search area, and the sun will be down in less than an hour. You said yourself that the ship seemed to be in okay condition, and I'm sure your brother will be okay, too."

"When that plane goes up, I want to be on it, okay?" Frank said in a quiet, determined manner.

"I think that can be arranged," she said. "Just don't give me a hard time while we're up there."

Frank laughed, even more impressed. "You mean, *you*—"

"Your pilot, at your service." She gave him a little salute. Then she checked her watch. "I get off in fifteen minutes. How about running back to the marina to shower and change, and meeting me at the café for a bite to eat in half an hour?"

"Only if it's my treat," Frank retorted. "Don't be late, though. I'm starved."

Dinner lasted late that night as Frank and Lieutenant Brown exchanged life stories. Lieutenant Brown told Frank about growing up on the coast of South Carolina. She came from a family of shrimp fishermen, she said. All her life she'd wanted to be one of the coast guard officers she'd seen cruising the ocean in their creased and pressed white uniforms. She had graduated from the academy just two years before, and San Juan was her first port.

Promising to pick him up before dawn, the lieutenant left Frank to spend the night in the cabin of the *Sun Dancer*.

When the sound of a honking horn woke him a few hours later, Frank leapt off his berth, pulled on shorts, a short-sleeved shirt, and sneakers and ran out to join Lieutenant Brown in her jeep. When daylight broke, they were over the ocean.

Arriving at the search area, Frank was dismayed to see that the entire region was covered by low clouds that touched down almost to sea level. "Don't worry, Frank," Lieutenant Brown said over the noise of the twin engine two-seater. She pointed to her radar screen. "We've still got eyes."

While Frank peered out the windshield, Lieutenant Brown swung the plane back and forth over a wide grid, staring into her radar screen for the blip that would indicate a ship below.

After three hours, Officer Brown told Frank, "We'll have to turn back. Otherwise, we're going to run out of fuel. We can try again this afternoon."

"What about search boats?" Frank shouted.

"At the moment there are none available—they're all out taking care of damage the storm brought in. Maybe tomorrow, if we're lucky."

If we're lucky! Frank thought anxiously. He couldn't imagine waiting another whole day.

29

Suddenly Frank saw a cluster of blips appear on the radar screen. "There!" he shouted.

"Nope." Lily shook her head. "That's a reef. A ship would be just one small blip on the screen."

Frank felt all the hope drain out of him.

"It doesn't mean they're not down there somewhere," Officer Brown said. "We might have calculated wrong."

Maybe, thought Frank, dejected. And maybe the *Laura Baines* had gone down in the storm. "Let's go down low," he urged her. "One last pass before we turn back."

"We won't see much," Lily pointed out. "But we'll give it a try." Giving him a smile, she pushed forward on the stick.

"I hear a plane!" Joe shouted. "Captain Evans, listen, can you hear it?"

The captain turned his face to the wind and stood very still on the bridge. "Yes," he said softly.

"There!" Joe pointed to a tiny silver dot nosing down through the cloud bank on the horizon. "They're too far away," he added. "And they're not headed in our direction!"

"The flares!" Captain Evans said urgently. "In the radio room. Hurry!"

Joe's heart hammered as he and the captain made their way to the radio room. It must be Frank! he thought. All Joe and the captain had to do now was alert the plane to their presence, and they'd be off the *Laura Baines* in no time.

Bursting into the radio room, Joe watched as the captain ripped open a cabinet. It was empty.

"Blast!" he shouted. "The flares were in here—three boxes of them!"

"You mean—" Joe's heart twisted in his chest.

"They're gone, boy. Those no-good villains swiped them. Every last one!"

Chapter

4

"SEARCH PLANE zero-four-two to base, do you read me, over?" Lieutenant Brown had taken the plane down below the cloud bank. Glancing at the altimeter, Frank saw that they were only a thousand feet above the ocean.

"We read you, zero-four-two," came a man's voice over the radio. "Come back in, Lily. You're going to run out of fuel. Over."

"Ten-four, Major," Lieutenant Brown replied. "Over and out." Putting down the mouthpiece, she turned to Frank. "Sorry, Frank. Up we go." She grabbed for the throttle, but just as she did so, Frank saw a hulking shape on the distant horizon.

"Hold it!" he cried out. "That looks like a ship over there!" He pointed, and Lily Brown swung the plane around. Soon they were circling over a dime-size rusty hull, nearly turned over on its side.

"That's her all right!" Frank said jubilantly. "I'd recognize that rust bucket anywhere!"

"I'll call in for a helicopter," Officer Brown said, relief apparent in her voice. "They'll be here within an hour. We can dip a wing to let them know we see them. Then is it okay if we go?"

"Anything you say, Officer," Frank said with a mock salute. They exchanged a grin. "Thanks," he added. "You've made my brother one very happy guy."

When Frank and the lieutenant entered the coast guard station less than an hour later, a short, slim man in a white major's uniform came out from behind the counter to join them. He looked to Frank to be in his midthirties, with short brown hair, dark eyes, and a confident, easygoing manner. "Major Rivera," said Lily, "this is Frank Hardy, brother of the boy on the ship. Frank, my boss."

Frank and the major shook hands. "Good work, Lily," the chief said, congratulating her. "Wait till you see what I have waiting in the holding room."

Rolling his eyes, he led them past the counter, through a door marked No Admittance, and down a long, empty hallway. A plate-glass window in the wall offered a view of a room where a dozen ragged men sat miserably on a long bench. "It's one-way glass," the chief said. "They can't see you."

"Who are they?" Frank asked.

"The crew of the *Laura Baines*," the major told a surprised Frank and Lily. "We picked them up this morning, drifting in a lifeboat. They claim there was a fire on board and the captain ordered them to abandon the ship. When the ship started taking on water, they did what he said. He wouldn't go with them, though. He insisted on going down with the ship."

"We didn't see anyone on deck," Frank heard Lily point out to the captain. "We were far away, though, so they might have been there."

"What kind of a captain goes down with a worthless old freighter?" the major asked, not really expecting an answer.

Frank gazed at the sailors. A short, burly, middle-aged seaman in filthy jeans and a T-shirt was standing and seemed to be arguing with a tall, stringy-haired younger man.

"Who's that guy?" Frank pointed at the middle-aged sailor, who was angrily pointing a cigar at the younger seaman. The others on the bench watched, and some of them were clearly egging the older sailor on.

"That's Vince Brewer," the major told him. "The captain's mate. He's been stirring up trouble with the others ever since we picked them up this morning. He tells us he's enforcing discipline. It sounds more like verbal abuse to me.''

"Yeah, you can tell by watching him." As Frank stared, Brewer glanced over his shoulder at the window. Frank knew he was behind one-way glass, but he could have sworn Vince Brewer stared right at him. He was surprised by the cold, bitter expression on the man's face.

"They're eight short," the major interjected. "We figure the other crew members are still drifting or, more likely, the fire or the storm got them."

Just then Frank watched as Vince Brewer pulled back his fist and punched the younger sailor. The rest of the crew circled them, shouting as the older sailor grabbed the young man's head, ready to smash it against the wall.

"Hey!" Major Rivera pounded on the window with his fist. The sailors slowly returned to their seats, except for Vince Brewer who glared at the one-way glass.

"I'll send someone in there to take care of him," the major snapped angrily, leading the way to the reception area. There, Frank saw Joe and an enormous man in a captain's uniform being led through the door by a young officer in coast guard white. Joe appeared to be exhausted as he approached the desk with the angry captain.

"Joe!" Frank shouted, running over to him.

"Frank!" Joe's face lit up when he saw his

brother. His blue eyes flicked over to Lieutenant Brown, then back to Frank again, while the major drew their young escort aside to instruct him to tend to the sailors. "Been keeping yourself busy, I see. Glad I was able to join you."

"Give me a break!" Frank gave his brother a mock punch on the arm. "I swore never to rest until you were found. Besides, Dad would have skinned me alive if you'd turned up with a single scratch on you."

"I'll vouch for Frank's efforts," Lily chimed in. "If Frank hadn't spotted your ship this morning, you guys might still be there."

Frank introduced Joe to Lieutenant Brown and Major Rivera, then Joe turned to present the tired captain. "The skipper of the *Laura Baines*," he announced. "Captain Daniel Evans. This man is a great navigator. He saved my life."

Frank shook the older man's hand. "Thank you, sir. Frank Hardy. I owe you one."

The captain nodded fiercely and faced Major Rivera. "Have they found my crew yet?" he demanded.

The major nodded. "We have twelve in custody. We're still searching for the others."

Captain Evans's black eyes smoldered. "Vince Brewer?" he whispered.

The major frowned. "He's back there. You can see him in a minute, if that's what you want.

But first, I'd like to hear your version of what happened.''

Rivera led the group into a conference room off the long hallway. Captain Evans proceeded to tell them the story of the fire and mutiny exactly as he had told it to Joe. Frank thought several parts of the story sounded fishy. Why would a crew desert a ship they wanted to take over, he wondered? And why would they set fire to it and flood the cargo holds?

When the captain had finished, the major informed him, "Brewer tells it differently, sir. He claims you ordered the crew off the ship, though it wasn't necessary. He says they might have been able to save the ship, but you went crazy. I have to tell you, Captain," Rivera added, looking straight into Evans's eyes, "those are some pretty heavy accusations—especially if we don't manage to save the rest of your crew. The other eleven men in the holding cell back Brewer up, too.''

Captain Evans scowled. "They would," he muttered. "How long were they out in that boat? Twenty-four hours is plenty of time to concoct a story and memorize it.''

"Let's bring Vince Brewer in and talk to him," said the major.

"There you are," the captain growled as an officer escorted Brewer into the room a few minutes later. "You slimy worm—you should have gone to the bottom as you deserved.''

"Right, Captain." Brewer, standing just inside the doorway, spat the words at the captain. With his bloodshot eyes and tattoos on his forearms, he looked even more threatening than he had in the other room.

The two men leapt at each other, and Major Rivera called for help from outside. Frank, Joe, and Lily watched as the captain landed a punch on Brewer's jaw, and Brewer returned it with a slam punch on the captain's nose that sent blood spurting into the air.

"Hey!" Joe yelled, starting to leap in to protect the captain from the first mate. Just then several officers appeared to separate the men.

"That will be enough!" Major Rivera snapped, glaring angrily at the two men. He handed the captain a handkerchief to stop his nosebleed, then said, "Let me tell you something—both of you. There are some serious accusations being thrown around here." He looked at Vince, who was sneering at the captain despite his bruised jaw. "If what Captain Evans says is true, Mr. Brewer, you and the rest of the crew are guilty of mutiny and abandoning ship. You'll be hauled before the maritime court and tossed out of the seamen's union. Not only that—I'll see you're charged with manslaughter in the deaths of any men we determine were drowned in this fiasco." Brewer glared sullenly at the major, without speaking.

"And you, Captain," the major continued, turning to Evans. "If this man is telling the truth, you'll be charged with criminal negligence and manslaughter. If you're declared sane, you could spend the rest of your life in prison."

Joe spoke up. "Major, I can vouch for Captain Evans. He tried hard to save the ship. I don't think anyone else could have beached the *Laura Baines* on that reef the way he did."

"Thanks, Joe," the major said soberly. Then he turned to the others in the room. "You can all go for now. But, Captain Evans, you and your crew are not to leave San Juan until we've completed our investigation. Joe Hardy, I'll need a statement from you. After that you can go where you want, but keep us informed of your whereabouts."

As the group filed out of the room, two officers held Brewer well out of range until the captain passed.

"I guess I'll head over to the Santa Maria Hotel on the waterfront," the captain said to Joe. "How would you and your brother like to join me for dinner?"

"Thanks, Captain." Joe glanced back at Brewer. "Maybe tomorrow. I'm really bushed, and besides, I want to call my parents."

"Until later, then." As the captain lumbered down the hall ahead of them, Frank glanced over his shoulder at the first mate. The look in Brewer's eyes spelled murder—and to Frank's horror, his eyes were aimed at Joe's head.

* * *

39

That night, after saying goodbye to Lieutenant Brown and telephoning their parents, the Hardys ate a quick dinner at the Club Nautico Café before heading back to the *Sun Dancer* for a good night's sleep.

"Lily said the inquiry at maritime court is scheduled for Thursday," Frank told his brother as they ambled down the pier in the moonlight. "Today's Friday. That means we have six days to solve this case—assuming that we want to get involved."

"Involved?" Joe ran a hand through his hair. "We already are involved, aren't we? I want to stay here to testify. The captain's depending on me."

"Joe, what makes you think the captain's telling the truth? His story's full of holes. If you ask me, neither of those guys is telling the truth."

"Give me a break," Joe protested. "One look at Brewer is enough to tell you he's up to no good. You should have seen the captain piloting that ship. It was like she was a part of his own body. He could no more destroy her than he could—"

"Okay, I get the point." Frank laughed, heading toward the *Sun Dancer,* moored several boats farther down the pier. "I should know better than to ask Joe Hardy to go against his instincts when—"

"Frank!" At the sound of Joe's voice, Frank

spun around to see a thick, hairy arm around his brother's neck. It was too dark to see who the attacker was, but he seemed to be shorter than Joe.

"Hey!" Frank said, starting forward. Before he could reach Joe, he was hit on the head from behind. With a cry, Frank crumpled to the floor. Blackness closed around him as he heard the faint sounds of a scuffle nearby. Then a handkerchief went over his mouth, and he smelled something sickeningly sweet.

"Frank!" he heard again, very far away now. Frank could no longer answer. The world had turned fuzzy, and he was falling fast asleep.

Frank opened his eyes to find himself on a hard, rocking surface under a full Caribbean moon. He blinked, realizing that his hands were tied behind his back. Joe lay beside him in the same position but still unconscious. They were on a boat, Frank realized. He looked around and saw that the craft was small and simple, like a fishing boat.

Frank breathed in the cool night air, struggling to shake off the cobwebs in his brain. He looked toward the horizon, but the lights of San Juan were nowhere to be seen. They were out at sea, he realized with a growing sense of dread.

Just then Frank heard footsteps approaching from behind. "Okay," a man said in a gruff voice that sounded vaguely familiar. "Let's get this over with." Frank narrowed his eyes to slits, pretending to be unconscious as a man with a black stocking pulled down over his face moved into view. Two other masked men soon joined the first. "Put them in the lifeboat," the first man said.

Frank was sure he recognized the short man's burly, muscular shape. He had to be Vince Brewer, though in a long-sleeved shirt, jeans, and mask Frank would find it hard to prove. Frank kept his eyes closed as the other two manhandled him into a small rowboat but flinched as one of the wooden seats slammed against his lower back. The bottom of the boat was hard and empty. A moment later Joe fell heavily on the floor beside him.

"Cast them off," Frank heard the first man say. The squeak of a pulley and a jolting sensation signaled their being lowered into the night-dark sea. Frank fought a surge of panic as a fresh ocean breeze circulated inside the rowboat. Water slapped against the boat, the ropes disengaged, and the tiny rowboat was left to drift.

"Okay!" Frank heard the masked man yell. He opened his eyes, no longer caring if anyone saw him awake.

Frank sat up in time to see the fishing boat steam off into the night. He looked down at his unconscious brother and kicked him in the side. "Joe, wake up!"

"Huh?" said Joe, coming to. "What's going on? Where are we?"

"How should I know?" Frank yelled, almost out of control as he realized there was no one anywhere near to hear them. "We're in the middle of nowhere! They've left us here to die!"

"DON'T WORRY, FRANK," Joe said several hours later as he sat waiting for the sun to come up. "We made it back to land already this week."

"Yeah, with the coast guard's help," Frank said angrily. "Now all we can do is watch a beautiful sunrise and hope that someone notices that we've disappeared. The way I figure, we've spent five hours so far in this dinky boat—the first four tied up. Six hours or so from now, the search will start, then a week or so from now— if we're lucky—a search plane might spot us."

"Whether anybody finds us or not, I have to know who did this to us," Joe said angrily. "The last thing I remember is a hairy arm around my neck—then bang! I was out for the count."

"They knocked us out with ether," Frank told

him impassively. "As to who it was—I figure it had to be Vince Brewer. He's bad news."

"Yeah," Joe agreed. His attention was caught by something on the horizon, and his face lit up. "All right!" he said, half-standing in the boat and waving his arms. "A boat! Stand up, Frank. We can't let it pass us by!"

Nearly half an hour later, as the small fishing trawler they had spotted chugged up to the boys' boat, Frank and Joe cheered.

"*Hola!*" called the pilot, a dark-haired man in old, stained jeans and a T-shirt.

Joe waited impatiently, eyeing the small rickety boat and the three fishermen on board, while Frank carried on a conversation with them in his high school Spanish. Soon the fishermen gestured for the Hardys to board their boat. After tying the rowboat to the back, the group began to chug home.

"They're from San Juan," Frank told his brother as the Hardys sat exchanging polite nods with the fishermen. "When we get back to the marina, pay them fifty dollars. They were following a school of fish, and I promised to pay them for the fish they didn't catch."

"Fifty dollars!" Joe stared at his brother. "Why don't you just give them the rowboat?"

"I want the coast guard to look it over," Frank replied. "Maybe they can figure out where it came from. Or maybe we can return it to Vince Brewer."

"Fine," Joe grumbled as San Juan appeared on the distant horizon. "But why do *I* have to pay for the ride?"

"Because I did the interpreting," Frank pointed out with a grin.

Two hours later Lieutenant Brown stood on the dock outside the coast guard office, looking down at the rowboat the Hardys had moored there. "Do you know how many of these boats there are in San Juan alone?" she asked them. "This one could have come from anywhere. You should report what happened to the police, but it's unlikely they'll be able to help you."

"But we practically saw the guy!" Joe protested. "He was short and built just like Vince Brewer, Captain Evans's first mate."

"Joe, the coast guard isn't allowed to investigate crimes that take place on land," Lily explained patiently. "Even if you had solid evidence, we couldn't question anyone for a mugging at the marina." She smiled. "Frank tells me you've both done a lot of detective work. Why don't you see what you can find out on your own?"

"We intend to," Frank said, his expression somber. "Meanwhile, if you turn up anything on this boat, please let us know."

"I promise," Lily agreed. Then she added tentatively, "I guess it isn't against the rules to tell you that we've done a background check on the crew. Brewer's the only one with a serious record—he got arrested for stealing cargo from a ship he worked on. Never came to trial, though." She glanced at Joe. "Captain Evans came out looking worse than anyone."

"Why?" Joe asked, surprised.

"Twelve years ago his license was suspended for ten years. He wrecked a cargo ship and was cited for gross negligence—and being an incompetent navigator."

Joe shook his head. "I watched him navigate that ship, Lieutenant. He's better than good. If he messed up back then—"

"It might have been on purpose?" Frank finished for him. "Maybe Captain Evans makes exceptions in certain cases. For the right price."

"Have you contacted the *Laura Baines*'s owner?" Joe asked Lily.

"Mr. Baines, the owner, is in the Philippines at the moment, and we haven't been able to locate him. His son Timothy was on the *Laura Baines*. He's missing—presumed dead.

"Maybe we'll find Timothy yet," Lily said. "We've found all the lifeboats—along with six more crew members since yesterday—but Timothy and the other missing crew member might have been washed up somewhere safe."

"Has the coast guard checked out the *Laura Baines* yet?" Frank asked.

"There's an inspection crew on its way there now," Lily answered. "I expect some insurance investigators will turn up soon enough, too."

"Insurance investigators?" Frank asked.

The lieutenant nodded. "Those big freighters might not look like much, but they're worth a bundle," she said. "The *Laura Baines* is probably insured for more than a million dollars. Alexander Baines should come into enough money to buy a brand-new ship—"

She was about to continue when an officer called to her, "Telephone, Lieutenant."

"We'll check in with you again later," Frank suggested. "Maybe we could all have dinner tonight. You could introduce us to more San Juan cuisine."

Lieutenant Brown smiled. "Give me a call this afternoon." As she ran toward the office, she added over her shoulder, "You guys had better get busy. Remember—the hearing's Thursday!"

"Where to first, Joe?" Frank asked after she'd gone.

"First a shower. Then we eat," Joe answered instantly.

Joe was relieved to learn that Club Nautico's lunch menu included double-decker hamburgers with french fries. He wolfed down two while Frank tried the sautéed shrimp and tossed salad. "Look at this scenery!" Joe said through a mouthful of burger as he poured ketchup on his french fries. "Blue skies, white surf, fantastic-looking women. If it weren't for getting kidnapped and being passed over by San Juan's prettiest lieutenant for my brother, I'd really be enjoying this break. What is it about you, Frank, that attracts brainy women?"

"Give me a break, Joe," Frank said with a laugh. "How long has it been since a girl paid more attention to me than you?"

"You have a point there." Joe readjusted his mirrored sunglasses. "I do remember a cute redhead who went after you when I was about four—"

"Excuse me. Joe Hardy?" A polite voice interrupted Joe, who turned to look at the speaker.

"That's me." He extended his hand to a tall, thin man in a light beige suit and fedora. The man had a narrow face with a pencil-thin mustache, and he eyed Joe with interest. "Who are you?" Joe asked.

"Percy Hughes-Smith." The man handed Joe a business card. "Bailey-Hopgood Maritime Insurance Company. We hold a policy on the *Laura Baines,* and I'm investigating the claim. I checked in with the coast guard office, and a very pretty lieutenant there suggested I talk with you."

Joe glanced at Frank. "Sit down, Mr. Hughes-Smith. Had your lunch?"

"Yes, thank you." The middle-aged man sat in the chair Joe indicated and took out a pad of paper and a pen. "I understand you were on board with Captain Evans," he explained. "I

49

was wondering if you'd tell me what shape it was in when you left."

"It sprang a leak while we were still out on open sea," he said. As Joe continued the story of his trip through the storm, and of Captain Evans's efforts to beach the ship, Hughes-Smith took notes.

"I see." The investigator sounded doubtful as he made a last note on the pad. "Some crew members said that the captain might have started the fire in the fore cargo hold. They say Evans acted crazily, ordering them to abandon ship while the fire was still controllable."

"You're taking the crew's word for that?" Joe said, irritated.

"My brother and I wouldn't know," Frank said calmly to the investigator. "We weren't there at the time."

"No. Of course not," Hughes-Smith said, clicking his ballpoint pen. "The captain generally is involved in cases of insurance fraud. It's easier that way—fewer people need know what's going on. And Captain Evans's past speaks for itself."

"You're sure it's fraud?" Frank asked.

Hughes-Smith shrugged. Joe interrupted before he could speak, "You can't hold Evans's record against him. Besides, that was twelve years ago."

"A lot of money is at stake here," the investigator said wearily. "Enough money to satisfy a shipowner *and* pay a captain off for life."

"Did you speak with the owner?" Frank demanded.

"We're looking for him." Hughes-Smith replaced the pad and pen in his pocket and stood up. "When we find him, you can be sure we'll have plenty of questions. Meanwhile, please don't hesitate to call if you remember anything more," he said to Joe. "Our company pays well for helpful information." Tipping his hat, the investigator walked away.

"What a geek," Joe muttered after Hughes-Smith was out of sight. "His company just doesn't want to pay off on the ship, that's all."

Frank stood up and put some money on the table for lunch. "We have things to do—like check out the offices of Alexander Baines and Company. If something fishy is going on, that's where it should smell the most."

Checking the San Juan phone book, Joe learned that the shipping company's offices were on the waterfront in the cargo area of the docks.

Joe was struck by the sudden change of atmosphere as they left the marina to approach the dock. Here, the marina's fluttering flags were replaced by piles of crates and rows of heavy forklifts and cranes. Frank checked the names on the office doors that fronted the single-story warehouses lining the water and stopped in front of one of them.

"Alexander Baines," he said, reading the brass plate beside the door. "Let's go."

They entered a small, nearly empty waiting room. Joe noticed that its grimy walls were decorated with faded posters of ships and framed photographs of a heavyset man—Alexander Baines, he guessed—receiving awards, dining with important people, and standing next to his wife. A metal desk covered with papers was placed near the door to an inner office. A clerk behind the desk spoke on the phone in rapid Spanish.

"Excuse me," Joe said, prompting an impatient, "Shhh!" from the clerk. Joe gave his brother a look that said, "It's up to you."

Frank waited until the clerk slammed the phone down. Then, as the clerk continued to ignore him, he said, *"Por favor?"*

Joe watched as Frank asked several carefully phrased questions in Spanish, but to each of them the clerk answered in a flurry of angry words and impatient gestures.

After a few minutes Frank motioned for Joe to follow him outside. He said to his brother, "We won't find out anything in there. Not from him, anyway."

"Why was he so mad?" Joe asked.

Frank shrugged. "I told him we were friends of Alexander's son Timothy and that we were looking for Tim's father. He acted like Timothy was the worst human being on the planet. I take it that father and son don't get along."

"Hmm," Joe said, then added philosophically, "better luck next time, I guess. Let's go."

"Wait," said Frank, grabbing Joe's arm. "Did you notice those papers on the guy's desk? They were bills. And you know what was stamped on nearly every one of them? 'Overdue.' 'Final Notice.' 'Urgent—Please Respond.' "

Joe nodded slowly. "So, Baines and Company may be about to go under. I bet Baines could really use a cool million to help pay those bills."

"If he did purposely set the ship up to be destroyed," Frank added, "someone on the *Laura Baines* must have helped. I hate to say it, Joe, but that makes your friend the captain a prime suspect again."

"I don't know, Frank. I have a feeling there are still pieces missing from this puzzle.

"Then, after dinner, we're coming back here. The clerk will be gone. And we'll have a quick look around the office."

An afternoon tour of the hotels close to the waterfront failed to turn up any guests who matched Vince Brewer's description—or at least the hotel clerks were unwilling to tell the boys if he was there. They tried to forget about Brewer as they accompanied Lily to her favorite restaurant that evening.

Lily told them that the investigating crew had returned from the *Laura Baines*. The freighter was in very bad condition—most of the cargo was underwater. It wasn't yet clear whether the fire had been deliberately set. The crew's report included the ship's cargo manifest, which described what the ship was carrying. "The *Laura Baines* had cotton, tropical hardwood, clothing, and a hundred crates of surplus U.S. Army munitions on board," she told the boys. "Our guys recommended that a full-fledged salvage crew be sent there as soon as possible."

"Army munitions!" Joe said. "That ship could have been blown sky-high during the fire—or later, when I was on it!"

"Our officers thought of that," Lily replied. "But the munitions were in the Numbers One and Two cargo holds, not Number Three. They were to be delivered to the army base in Puerto Rico."

"Wouldn't that usually be done by navy ships?" Frank asked her.

"The army sometimes contracts with private companies," Lily replied. "We're checking into it, though." Lily then changed the subject, and the Hardys were soon laughing at stories of her many misadventures at the Coast Guard Academy.

After Lily had dropped the boys off at the marina, the Hardys headed back to the warehouse district. The marina had been crowded with tourists on their way to dance clubs and parties, and music wafted out from small cafés along the nearby sidewalks. The warehouse district was a grimmer, more dangerous world. Even in the dark Joe could identify it by the smells of fish and produce stored inside the buildings.

"Hold it." Frank stopped as they approached the side of the Baines and Company warehouse. The boys watched as a truck backed up to the Baines loading dock. Two men, illuminated by a streetlamp, started carrying crates from the truck through the back door of the warehouse. Joe and Frank watched until one of the men locked the truck's doors, leaving the warehouse unlocked, and took off with his companion for a small café down the block.

"Now's our chance," Frank said. Joe followed him quietly into the warehouse and switched on his penlight.

The brothers moved toward the far wall, where a door led to the front offices. Joe trained his light on the door while Frank tried the knob. "It's open, too," Frank said.

Joe shone his light around the main office. The walls were lined with filing cabinets and shelves, and the room had a musty smell. "This must be where they keep the records and manifests," he heard his brother say as Frank began opening the filing drawers, one after the other. "Hey, this drawer's locked." He tried several others. "It's the only one that's locked."

"You've got your lock pick," Joe said.

"Sure thing." In seconds the file drawer was opened and Frank was flipping through to a folder marked *"Laura Baines."*

"Shine the light here," Frank said, pointing. "Look—this one's from the Department of Transport. 'Upon arrival in San Juan and discharge of her cargo, the *Laura Baines* is to be scrapped. The ship's Certificate of Seaworthiness cannot be renewed.' "

"Wow," Joe said. "That means if Captain Evans had brought her to port, she would be worth only the price of her scrap metal!"

"But if she sank, she'd be worth a million dollars," Frank concluded. "Things are looking worse for Alexander Baines."

Just then Joe heard voices in the warehouse area outside the office. "They're back!" he whispered. "They must have just gone for coffee." He flipped off his light.

"Good thing we closed the door." Frank slipped the file back in the cabinet. "We'll wait for them to leave. Then we'll go."

Joe backed away from the door. He tripped over a trash can and stumbled into the file cabinets.

"Whoa!" he shouted involuntarily as notebooks, ledgers, and papers tumbled down on him from the top of the cabinets.

"Are you okay, Joe?" Frank asked under

his breath. "I hope so, because here comes trouble!"

Almost before Frank finished speaking, the office door flew open and the room was filled with blinding light. "Hey!" a voice roared over Joe's head. "What are you kids doing here?"

the mouth. "I have no intention of harming them
inside.
Now that wall was chucked operating, there,
the board the wan and the room was silent with
sliding stain. "Hey," a voice for the two lads
even. "What are you like doing here?"

Chapter

6

"RUN, FRANK!" Joe exploded up and out from
beneath the pile of papers and threw himself at
the intruder, hitting him in the abdomen. With a
surprised grunt, the man doubled over, his flashlight flying. He tried to regain his balance but
slipped on the papers that littered the floor.

Joe sprinted out the door after Frank, who had
tangled with the first man's companion and was
on the floor with him.

Joe pulled the man off Frank and sent a fist
to his chin to knock him out. "Let's go," Joe
said to his brother, "before that other guy calls
for reinforcements."

As the brothers raced out of the warehouse
and back toward the marina, they heard running
footsteps behind them. A shot rang out, and Joe

saw a metal garbage can on the sidewalk to his left go flying. "Faster!" he gasped to Frank as they ran past dark buildings and empty streets. A moment later they were safely hidden among the throngs of tourists strolling along the piers of the marina.

"He wouldn't dare come after us here," Frank said as they slowed to a walk.

The brothers paused outside the boundaries of Club Nautico's marina and glanced back over their shoulders for their pursuer. "Who were those guys?" Joe asked. "And what were they loading into Alexander Baines's warehouse at night?"

Frank shook his head wearily. "It wasn't Vince Brewer, that's for sure. I never saw either of them before. This case gets weirder and weirder. I'd think it was a simple case of insurance fraud if—"

"If Alexander Baines weren't missing," Joe finished for him. "If two guys weren't unloading unidentified merchandise into Baines's warehouse at night. If Baines's own son hadn't been on board when the ship caught fire."

Frank nodded. "That's a lot of activity surrounding one broken-down freighter."

"The coast guard hasn't come up with anything helpful yet," Joe reminded him. "I say we go for a sail tomorrow and pay a call on the *Laura Baines*."

"Good idea," Frank replied. "But for now,

it's shut-eye time. I have a feeling the *Sun Dancer*'s going to rock me right to sleep."

The next morning Joe climbed onto the deck of the sailboat to find the weather hot and clear. After a quick breakfast, he and Frank cast off, unfurling the sails in the breeze. Joe noticed that the swells were high, but he wasn't worried. The *Sun Dancer* was a plucky little boat.

Joe directed Frank toward the reef, and soon the sloop was easing into the leeward shelter where the *Laura Baines* lay like a beached whale.

"I can see why navigators have nightmares about this place," Frank said. Throwing the anchor over the side, he added, "Got the dinghy ready?"

Joe finished pumping the rubber raft full of air. "Ready." He grabbed a paddle and handed one to Frank. Together they lowered the boat over the side. "Here we go."

The little craft swayed dangerously as they climbed in, but soon Joe and Frank were making progress against the swells, which, they noticed, were high even in the shelter of the reef. They were shocked to see that the main deck was now at sea level. Most of the port side of the ship, as well as the entire stern, had sunk into the sea.

"Looks like we made it just in time," Frank said. "Where do we go first?"

"The coast guard will have already been

through the bridge and the captain's and crew's quarters,'' Joe pointed out. "Let's try the chart room to see what we can find."

"Good idea." Joe led Frank onto the ship. It was difficult to move around because the ship lay at such an odd angle, rocking as the waves crashed against it. The boys almost had to walk sideways on the stairs, pulling themselves up the railings.

Moving behind the bridge, the boys entered a tiny room in which a large table stood covered with nautical charts. Frank approached the table, uphill, and studied the charts' markings. "The ship headed straight from the Philippines to Panama," he said, "through Colón on the Caribbean side of the Panama Canal, then northeast toward Puerto Rico. Nothing strange about that."

"Nothing here, either." Joe was searching the rows of drawers in cabinets along the downhill wall. He pulled out the top drawer of the farthest cabinet and reached behind a stack of charts that were stored there. "What's this?" He pulled out a large book. "It looks like the captain's log."

Frank crossed to look over Joe's shoulder. "That should contain the details of this past trip," he said as Joe turned the pages. "Look, this refers to a storm in the Pacific. 'The ship is strained and leaking. The pumps seem able to keep pace with the leakage. Situation is under control, for the moment. However, a risky passage lies ahead. I remain convinced, as I was in

Manila, that we should never have undertaken this voyage.' "

Joe turned a page, and a telegram dropped out onto the floor. He picked it up and read. " 'To A. Baines, Manila, from D. Evans, Panama: Sir—stop—ship in need of immediate repairs—stop—To proceed to San Juan otherwise not advisable—stop—Await your orders—stop.' "

"Here's another one." Frank pulled a telegram out of the logbook. "It looks like Baines's reply: 'No repairs are to be made unless absolutely essential—stop.' " Frank said dryly, "So Evans took her out knowing she was in lousy condition. This will look bad in maritime court."

"He would have lost his job if he hadn't," Joe argued. "He was right, too. The ship ran fine until the fire and the flood."

"We don't know that," Frank pointed out. "One thing that's clear is that Evans requested that the repairs be made. He wouldn't have done that if he'd planned to sink the ship."

"Right!" Joe said, brightening. "That proves my point."

"Or he might have sent the telegram to cover himself in case things went wrong," Frank said.

Frank took the book from Joe and turned back to the place where his brother had stopped reading. "That's weird." He showed Joe the page. "Two days of entries are missing."

Joe frowned. "What do you think that means?"

"I don't know," Frank said, "but I bet it's important."

"Come on," Joe said after an uncomfortable pause. "Let's check out the crew's quarters."

Joe led the way belowdecks to the crew's quarters. Nothing seemed suspicious. "Baines's cabin must be down the hall," he said. "Let's have a look."

Joe led Frank past the next few vacant cabins until they saw one that had been recently occupied. A jacket dangled off the back of a chair, and books, some still stacked on the berth, had fallen to the floor with papers from the desktop.

"What's this?" Frank picked up some pieces of paper from the floor. "A map of some kind." He peered closer. "It's of an island named San Xavier," he told Joe. "It's off the east coast of Central America."

"Anything marked on it?" Joe asked.

"There's a star on the island's southern shore, with 'Santa Marta' written next to it. That must be the capital. And then there are a few groups of *X*'s here and there on the island. Don't know what they mean. I have some stamps from San Xavier. It's such a tiny country that they're real collectors' items."

"What else is there?" asked Joe, trying to peer at the papers in Frank's hand.

"Stationery with Timothy Baines's name on it." Frank riffled through the papers. "And here's a list of Spanish names—a roster of some kind."

Joe shrugged. "Maybe he was doing some kind of research. Come on, there's nothing to look at here. Let's head for the Number One and Two cargo holds. I want to see those army munitions."

The boys made their way down to the rear holds, only to find that even the hatches were underwater. "We'll need scuba gear to get in there," Joe said. "At least the munitions won't blow up if they're soaking wet."

"Why don't we check out Number Three, then, where the fire broke out?" said Frank.

The Hardys made their way carefully toward the front of the ship, trying to keep their balance on the precarious angle as the freighter rocked back and forth. The waves must be growing larger, Joe noticed as they reached the hold's heavy steel door. He wiped his forehead with the sleeve of his T-shirt. It was hot.

"One, two, three!" Frank chanted as the brothers threw their combined strength into opening the heavy door. "The fire must have warped the metal," Frank remarked as they staggered into the large, dark room. They stood gazing around at the charred wreckage.

"Wow," said Joe. "Must have been some fire."

Before Frank could answer, a large wave hit the ship, and the freighter gave a sudden heave.

The boys were pitched forward. As they struggled to their knees, they heard the metal door clang shut. The hold was plunged into total darkness. Joe reached for his flashlight—it was gone, fallen out of his pocket.

"Frank!" Joe shouted, fighting the panic that rose in his chest. He felt for the door, then tried to pull it open.

"I'm right here." Joe heard Frank's voice beside him. "Let me try."

"It's no use!" Joe yelled. "The door's jammed. We're trapped inside!"

Chapter
7

"MOVE OVER," Frank said. "Let me try." The door didn't budge. "Great," said Frank. "Now what?"

"Hey, look," he heard Joe say. "That hatch, where they load the cargo in. See the light coming through?"

As Frank's eyes began to adjust, he could see light filtering in around a circle in the ceiling. "I see it," he said. "But how are we going to get that hatch cover open?"

"Do you see a ladder?" Joe asked. The boys inched across the room, trying not to stumble over the charred debris as they felt for a ladder. "We're going to look like coal miners when we get out of here," Joe muttered.

Handing Joe the logbook he'd held on to,

Frank made his way up the ladder, which was secured to a beam. With each swell of the ocean, he had to pause and cling tightly to the ladder.

At the top Frank let go with one hand and reached out toward the hatch, a good eight feet away. "Here goes nothing," he said. Just as he touched the hatch, a swell knocked hard against the ship, causing the freighter to shift position.

"Whoa!" Frank yelled as the ladder pulled away from the beam. "Jump, Joe!" Backing quickly down the ladder, Frank half jumped, half fell to the bottom of the hold. The ladder tumbled sideways against a wall with an ear-shattering crash.

"Any more great ideas?" Frank asked as he sat huddled next to Joe on the floor.

"Not at the moment," he heard Joe reply. "Right now, I think I'm getting sick."

Frank looked around. By now he could just make out a few dim shapes in the hold. "How about stacking some of that cargo up to the hatch?" he suggested.

"Sounds good." Frank heard Joe struggle sluggishly to his feet. Together, the Hardys stacked half-burned bales of cotton into a tower. Then Frank heard Joe say, "What's that smell? Hey, look, Frank," Joe said. "It's a barrel, and it smells like it had kerosene in it."

Frank joined his brother and sniffed at the empty barrel. "You're right, Joe. The coast guard guys must have thought it was just some of the cargo. You know what this means, don't you?''

"Arson," Joe replied.

Frank nodded. "Let's get out of here."

With great difficulty, the Hardys managed to stack the cotton bales high enough for Frank to climb up to the hatch. Five minutes later he'd released the handle and raised the cover, and the Hardys climbed through.

Back on the main deck Frank checked out his brother and laughed. "Somebody ought to toss you right into the washing machine," he joked.

Joe wiped a hand across his face and inspected the grime on his palm. "I wonder if ash is good protection against sunburn?" he asked.

Frank chuckled. "We'll find out. Let's get back on the *Sun Dancer*. I want to report this to Lily right away."

When they reached the sloop and turned on the radio, all Frank could hear was static. "We're out of range," he told Joe. "We'll have to sail back and tell Lily in person."

"It's tough being a good citizen, isn't it?" Joe kidded as he washed the soot off his face with a cloth. "I just have to admire you."

"We went out to the *Laura Baines* to investigate this morning, and we have some news for you," Frank said to Lily Brown when they got to the coast guard office.

"Great," Lily said, lowering her voice and

leaning over the counter. "I have news, too. Vince Brewer was brought in for questioning again today. He gave Major Rivera plenty to think about."

"Like what?" Frank asked.

"Like the fact that the *Laura Baines* was Alexander Baines's last ship," Lily told him. "And that the whole crew knew the freighter was to be scrapped any day. A lot of the guys were mad, Brewer said, because they were about to lose their jobs, but they didn't dare complain much because Alexander's son was on board."

"Is that all?" Joe asked.

"Nope," Lily told him. "He also said that Baines's shipping company has been operating at a loss ever since Alexander split up with his brother, Max, three years ago. Max Baines has six top-of-the-line freighters. He's supposed to be a genius at making money. Brewer said the brothers split because Alex couldn't stand playing second fiddle to Max. Too bad for Alex—his brother may have been keeping him afloat."

"I wonder how much of it is true," Frank said thoughtfully. "I wish I could have been here for the questioning."

"You've poked your nose around enough, don't you think?" Lily said. "We have a salvage crew heading for the *Laura Baines* right now. Do you think there's anything left for them to salvage?"

"I doubt it," Frank said lightly. He handed her the logbook. "Your men overlooked this yesterday. There are a couple of pages missing—Major Rivera should find that fascinating.''

"There was a barrel with kerosene hidden in the hold where the fire started, too," Joe volunteered. "The salvage crew will probably find it."

"Have you heard anything about the missing crew members or Timothy Baines?" Joe asked.

Lily shook her head sadly. "We're still combing the area," she told him, "but we're about to stop the search." She sighed. "Where are you two headed now?"

"The Santa Maria Hotel," Frank heard Joe say. "That's where Captain Evans said he'd be staying. I think it's time Frank heard his side of the story."

"Good luck," Lily said, tossing Frank a smile. "The Santa Maria's no five-star resort."

Frank and Joe walked to the waterfront and the hotel, following Lily's directions. "There it is," Joe said, pointing down the street to an old narrow colonial-style building sandwiched between two shorter, newer edifices. The pink paint was flaking off the hotel facade. The second-story balcony hung at a dangerous slant, and the front porch and lobby were occupied by dull characters gazing blankly out at the dusty street.

"Buenas tardes," Frank said politely, approaching a very fat man who sat watching television behind the counter. *"El Cápitan Evans está aquí?"*

70

"Yeah, over there in the corner," the man said with an American accent. He pointed the captain out to the Hardys, then went back to his show.

"Hello there, lads!" The captain greeted the boys as they joined him in a small alcove, where he sat playing solitaire. It made Frank sad to see him by himself, ignored even by the derelicts who occupied the same hotel. "Come to say goodbye?"

"What do you mean?" Joe asked.

"They'll be locking me up after this, I reckon," said the older man with a sigh.

"We'd like to ask you a few questions," Joe said. "Maybe we can help you get out of this mess."

"Ask away," said the captain. "But it won't do any good. They framed me once before, and I couldn't beat that one. And now, with one black mark on my record, what chance do I have?"

"What about that black mark?" Frank asked. "Why do you say you were framed?"

"Because it's the truth, son!" The captain slammed a queen of hearts down on the table. "Curly MacDougal, the mate on the ship I captained back then, falsified the charts, then claimed it was my error." He turned to Joe. "I can tell you now what must have happened—MacDougal must have been paid off by the owners to wreck the ship. When I was blamed for doing a lousy

71

job, the insurance company had to pay the money. The owners made a killing, and I took the fall. Those lawyers carved me up like a roast pig." He heaved a deep sigh.

"But Alexander Baines wouldn't have wrecked his ship with his own son on board," Frank objected.

"You don't think so?" the captain said bitterly. "You don't know how much those two hate each other then!" The captain slapped down his cards. "I tell you, that Tim Baines is a bad one," he confided. "Just like his uncle Max. He was a bad deed waiting to happen. But Alex Baines—" He shook his head grimly. "I have to admit, what he's done surprises me."

"Did Tim Baines often travel on the ship?" Frank asked.

Evans shrugged. "We hadn't seen him for over a year before this last time—not since his poor mother died. I wondered why he showed up all of a sudden. He seemed excited, too— like he had some kind of project going that he was keeping secret. He spent a lot of time in his cabin—planning his future, he said. I guess whatever he was up to, none of us'll ever know now."

Frank frowned. So far, the information Evans had given them wasn't much. "I have a confession to make, Captain," he said. "My brother and I sailed out to the *Laura Baines* this morning and we found your log. Entries for two days are missing. Do you know what could have happened to them?''

The captain smiled wanly. ''Oh, that,'' he said. ''I'll plead guilty to that one. Those two days were a blur for me, lads. I was in a hospital in Panama City. My stomach. While I was out, my mate tried to fill in the log for me. He botched the job up so badly that when I read those pages I ripped them out in front of him.'' He shrugged apologetically. ''I forget myself at times.''

''What was wrong with your stomach?'' Joe piped up. ''Bad food?''

''Excellent food!'' the captain replied. ''The night before, I was wined and dined by Max Baines himself. Fresh lobster on his newest ship, the *Northern Star*.''

''Max Baines was in Panama at the same time the *Laura Baines* was?'' Frank asked, surprised. ''Quite a coincidence, don't you think?''

''Not at all. His ships are always going through the canal, one way or the other. He's a rat, Max Baines is, but he had no reason to poison old Dan Evans. Or to sink his brother's last ship either, come to that.'' The captain laughed. ''Max-a-million Baines, we used to call him. Funny, eh?''

A short time later the brothers walked out into the late-afternoon sunshine. ''I see why you've been defending him,'' Frank said to his brother.

73

"He's quite a character—and I can't really imagine him sinking his ship for money."

"Neither can I," said Joe. "That's why I want to get hold of Vince Brewer. If we can just talk to him for five minutes, we might be able to—"

Joe's voice was drowned out by the sudden roar of an engine. Turning, Frank saw a forklift, its forks raised, moving at top speed across the pavement right toward him and Joe. Frank tried to see the driver's face, but the sun was shining in his eyes.

"Watch out, Frank!" he heard Joe yell as he ran off to the right. After a few steps he turned to watch the forklift speeding after Joe.

"Help!" Joe yelled. He was trapped against a stack of crates piled next to a pier.

Frank began running toward his brother. But before Joe could move, the green vehicle plunged forward again, its twin blades aimed at Joe's chest.

"Frank!" Joe yelled. "He's got me!"

Chapter

8

JOE STARED, stunned, as the forklift closed the narrow gap to him. Time seemed to slow down as the two blades plowed forward on either side and smashed into the pile of crates behind him.

He opened his eyes. "I'm okay," he said, reassuring himself.

"Move it, Joe!" Frank's voice filtered through Joe's dazed consciousness. Moving instinctively he ducked under the blades and took off before the driver could get free of the crates and attack again.

"Did you get a good look at him?" Frank asked as he joined his brother.

"No, I couldn't identify the guy in his mirrored sunglasses and cap. But from his size, I'd guess it was Brewer again."

"He must really be afraid of your testimony," Frank said, shaking his head.

"Testimony? He'd better be afraid that I'll punch his lights out!" Joe growled.

Frank clapped a weary arm around his brother's shoulders. "Let's get back to Club Nautico as fast as we can. I want a four-course meal and eight hours' sleep. It's lucky there's extra security at the marina now. I think I'll be able to relax and sleep."

Joe and Frank felt better the next morning. By eight o'clock they were wolfing down breakfast at the café while Frank scanned the local newspaper.

"Hey," said Frank, reading a notice in the paper. "Listen to this: 'Memorial service for Timothy Baines, son of shipping executive Alexander Baines, to be held this morning at Seamen's Hall, ten A.M.' "

"That's weird," Joe said, gulping down his orange juice. "I didn't know they'd given up searching for him. With his father unavailable and his mother dead, who arranged a memorial service?"

Frank folded the paper. "Let's go find out."

"Looks like everyone showed up," Joe remarked, peering out the window as the taxi pulled up to the front of Seamen's Hall. The wide front steps of the colonial-style building held several dozen people. "I didn't know Tim was so popular."

As they climbed out of the taxi, Joe noticed Percy Hughes-Smith, the insurance investigator. "Hi," he called to the tall, thin man. "We didn't expect to see you here."

"Hello, boys," the investigator said, tipping his hat to the Hardys. "I read about the service in the paper this morning, and since my plane doesn't leave until this evening, I thought I'd drop in."

"You've finished your investigation so soon?" Joe asked as the three climbed the steps together.

"Not at all." The investigator entered the large hall ahead of the Hardys. "I received a call from Mr. Max Baines this morning. He informed me that his brother, Alex, is still in the Philippines, too grief-stricken by his son's death to deal with the collapse of his company. He's turned the business over to Max, who's decided under the circumstances to withdraw the insurance claim on the freighter. He agrees with us, you see," Hughes-Smith concluded with a self-satisfied smile. "There were suspicious activities connected with the *Laura Baines*'s sudden collapse. He doesn't want his own company sullied by any hint of scandal."

Joe said thoughtfully. "I thought Max and Alex Baines were enemies."

"That's not my business." Hughes-Smith dismissed Joe's comment with a flick of his hand.

The investigator moved to the front of the large meeting room, and the Hardys took seats near the back where they could watch the other guests. "That was a surprise," Joe said, commenting on what Hughes-Smith had told them. "Does this mean there was no insurance scam, or does it just mean that Max Baines is too rich to bother continuing a scam his brother started? And why would Alex give his company to a brother he hates, no matter how upset he is?"

"I have another question," Frank said casually. "If Alex Baines is so grief-stricken over Tim's death, why isn't he here? And if he isn't so grief-stricken, why is Max acting on his behalf? And if Alex was really trying to steal the insurance money in the first place, why wasn't he here instead of in the Philippines when he was most needed to stake his claim to the money?"

"Who knows?" Joe said gloomily. "This case is getting too murky for me."

"There's Vince Brewer," Frank said.

Joe spotted Brewer in the second row, surrounded by other members of the *Laura Baines*'s crew. Joe stared at him. "He doesn't exactly look like I remembered," he said to his brother. "Maybe he's not the guy who's been after us after all."

Joe turned to watch a large man in an expensive

white suit walk up the center aisle, followed by several men in ship officers' uniforms. Joe noticed his strong resemblance to the photographs of Alexander Baines in the shipping company's office.

"Max Baines!" he overheard an onlooker murmur to a friend in the row behind the Hardys. "He's Tim's uncle. He and Tim were like father and son the past year, since Tim's mother died. The boy blamed his dad for the mother's death, I hear. If that boy had lived, he would have inherited all Max Baines's money."

Joe's head was so full of questions that he found it impossible to pay attention to the ceremony. The instant the service was over, Joe stood up to go. "I'm going to follow Max Baines," he murmured to Frank. "You try to talk to Vince Brewer before he leaves here. I don't trust myself near that guy. I'm afraid I'll haul off and punch him."

"Got you," Frank agreed. Joe made his way back out into the blinding sunlight, where he stood watch as the crowd poured out of the hall.

As Joe hailed a taxi to follow the white Rolls-Royce that had whisked Max Baines away from the hall, Frank edged through the crowd on the front steps toward Brewer, who was leaving with several of his friends from the *Laura Baines*.

"Excuse me—Mr. Brewer?" Frank said as politely as he could. Brewer glanced at Frank and did a double take, then stopped and eyed him suspiciously.

"What do you want?" he said out of the corner of his mouth.

What did he want? Frank wanted to know if Vince Brewer had kidnapped him and left him for dead in the middle of the Caribbean. And whether he'd attacked Joe with a forklift last night. And whether he'd set fire to the *Laura Baines* because someone had paid him to and was now trying to frame Captain Evans. But at the moment Frank couldn't ask those questions.

"I was wondering how well you knew Tim Baines," Frank said lamely. "And how well he knew Captain Evans."

"Look, who are you?" Brewer asked impatiently. "I talked to the coast guard twice already. I don't have to talk to you. If you want to know about Tim Baines, go talk to his uncle," he added as he and his pals turned to go. "Those two were thick as thieves in Panama. Ask Max how come his nephew died this week."

Before Frank could respond, Brewer stalked off. Frank frowned, thinking over what Vince had said. Brewer seemed more angry than threatening, he realized. Frank began to doubt that he was the one who'd been attacking them. But if it wasn't Vince Brewer, he thought wearily, that puts us back at square one.

Hoping Joe had had better luck, Frank hopped a cab for the marina.

* * *

Joe was already at their usual table at the café when Frank arrived a few minutes later. He had a small pair of binoculars on the table beside him.

"I got these off the *Sun Dancer*." Joe handed over the binoculars as Frank sat down. "Check out Max's boat," he said, pointing.

Frank sat down and trained the binoculars on the magnificent yacht that Joe had indicated—a seventy-foot luxury craft tied up to one of the docks. "*Megabucks*," Frank said, reading the name painted in gold letters on the stern. He laughed. Then he saw the name of the home port painted underneath. "Santa Marta." He lowered the binoculars. "Joe, Santa Marta's the name of the city on that map in Tim's cabin."

"I know." Joe plucked the orange slice from his fruit punch. "Think there's some connection?"

"Maybe. But what?" Bewildered, Frank watched as three well-dressed men in business suits and sunglasses boarded the ship. Max Baines came into view, smoking a huge cigar. He greeted the men and ushered them to the foredeck, where there were chairs and tables.

Frank and Joe watched as the men sat down and drinks were served. Then one of the visitors pulled a fat envelope from his pocket and handed it to Max Baines.

"What's that?" Frank said as he watched Baines peek inside the envelope, then leave the deck and descend briefly into the cabin. When he returned, he no longer had the envelope in his hand. "It looks like Baines just got paid off, unless my eyes deceive me," he told Joe.

"Did you see green?" Joe asked.

"Nope. Just an envelope," Frank replied. "But I smell green. Something's up, Joe. I'm going to find out what. Our snorkeling equipment's still on the *Sun Dancer,* right? I'm going to swim up behind the ship and see what I can overhear."

"Sounds crazy," said Joe, "but if you're game, I'll help."

As the brothers moved quickly down the pier to their sloop, they saw Max Baines leave his boat and climb into a waiting car. "So what?" Frank said. "We can still go ahead with the plan. Maybe we'll learn something anyway."

It took only fifteen minutes for Frank to don his snorkeling gear and slip into the oily water of the marina. While Joe watched from the *Sun Dancer,* Frank moved quietly along the outside of the row of docked boats until he was within sight of the *Megabucks'*s stern. He dove underwater and surfaced right behind the yacht.

The engine of the *Megabucks* was idling, but Frank could hear voices over its drone. They sounded to Frank like a couple of crew members, gossiping in Spanish. From what he could make out, the men were talking about a *revolución* that was going to take place soon, and about *municiónes*—munitions. Frank heard the words *el jefe,* or "the boss," and then Max Baines's name was mentioned, along with his cargo ship, the *Northern Star.* Frank couldn't figure out what it all added up to, and he didn't have time to try.

With a sudden roar and a puff of noxious blue diesel fuel the engine sprang to life. The propeller, which had been idling, now spun full-speed as the ship began to back out of its berth.

Frank felt himself being dragged toward the razor-sharp blades. He struggled furiously against the current created by the propeller, but it was no use. He was being sucked in closer and closer. In seconds he would be drawn into the blades!

Chapter

9

FRANTICALLY, Frank tried to swim out of the powerful whirlpool. As fast as he could go, though, the boat, its propeller blades churning, kept moving closer and closer.

Then, at the last possible safe moment, the ship itself gave him a boost. The stern turned away from the dock, sending a little swell toward Frank. At the same instant the propeller's sucking force lessened as it moved away from him. With a quick burst, spending the last of his breath and energy, Frank rode the swell, grasping for one of the canvas bumpers that ringed the dock.

There! He made it. His throat made a loud gasping sound as he sucked in just enough air to keep from passing out. Slowly the ship backed out past him and moved away.

"Joe!" Frank shouted. "Help me out!"

Joe came running over from the *Sun Dancer*. He tossed Frank a rope to haul him out of the water and onto the dock. "That was a close one," Frank said as he recovered.

"Did you hear anything?" Joe asked. Frank related what he had heard. "Not bad," Joe said when he had finished. "Revolutions, huh? You don't think the munitions part could have anything to do with the munitions on the *Laura Baines,* do you?"

"I was wondering that myself," Frank said, "before I nearly drowned, that is. After all, it is weird that Max Baines showed up here when Alex Baines is still gone."

"Maybe Max is selling Alex's munitions cargo— though I have to admit it sounds pretty far-fetched," Joe said. "I think we'd better go talk to Lily Brown."

After changing clothes, Frank accompanied Joe to coast guard headquarters. Lily listened, frowning, while Frank told her about the conversation he'd overheard.

"This sounds serious," she said. "I'll suggest to Major Rivera that he ask the army's permission to move those munitions out of the freighter before anyone else does."

"But they're underwater," Joe broke in. "What use could they be now?"

"Guns are usually packed in grease to protect

them, in addition to the watertight crates they're stored in," Lieutenant Brown told him. "As for ammunition, even if it got wet, it might be usable once it dried out." She spoke to Major Rivera for a brief moment. After hanging up the phone, she told the brothers, "The major has agreed to contact the army. I'll let you know what happens."

"Do you really think Max Baines is selling the cargo off his brother's sinking ship?" Frank asked skeptically. "How would he know what was in the cargo holds? He and his brother don't even speak to each other."

"Maybe Tim told him," Lily suggested. "Or even Captain Evans, in a weak moment."

"I don't believe Evans would spill that kind of information," Joe said. "We should concentrate on figuring out who started the fire on board the *Laura Baines*."

The phone rang. "Yes, sir," Lily said several times, and then hung up. "That was the major," she told the Hardys. "Our frogmen are going to remove the crates one at a time. He's put me in charge of the operation."

Frank leaned forward. "Can we go along? We're experienced scuba divers, and we already know where the cargo is."

Lily considered for a moment. "Okay," she decided. "We could use your help. The cutter will be ready first thing in the morning. See you at the dock."

* * *

Frank and Joe arrived on time to meet Lily Brown and Major Rivera at the coast guard dock.

"Morning, boys." Rivera shook their hands. "I hear you've been doing some investigating. I got a call from the police yesterday. You were trespassing at Alexander Baines and Company, weren't you?"

"Who reported us?" Frank asked in surprise. Behind Rivera, a pair of divers were loading equipment on board the boat. Half a dozen crewmen were already on the deck of the cutter, ready to leave.

"The two workers you attacked," the major said. "They told the police they were unloading a shipment into the Baines warehouse when they stumbled on two teenage prowlers in the offices. I guessed from their descriptions that it might be you. The police aren't too happy about it, but I managed to put them off. Just cool it with the sneaky stuff, okay?"

"Yes, sir," Frank said, embarrassed. "We thought *those* two guys were criminals. It won't happen again." Frank decided not to mention the forklift incident. In light of the munitions stealing, it seemed pretty minor.

The major's face relaxed. "Good," he said. "Meanwhile, I want to thank you for your help with the investigation. The captain's log has been a big help. Lieutenant Brown says you want to go along today. I've given my permission."

"Thanks, sir," Frank said eagerly.

Major Rivera nodded. "By the way, the hearing on the *Laura Baines*'s sinking has been put off until Monday, so we'll have time to go over all the evidence before the trial."

"Great," Joe muttered to his brother after the major had returned to his office. "Six more days for Vince to try to kill me before I testify."

It was late morning by the time the coast guard cutter reached the reef. Frank stood on deck, letting the salt spray cool his face and enjoying the clear, cloudless weather. But the swells were quite high, especially around the reef. "Storm coming," Lily Brown said, sniffing the wind.

"Looks fine to me," said Joe, handing Frank his scuba gear. He sat down to begin putting on his own equipment. In the back of the boat, the two frogmen had already suited up. "Blazing sun, cool breeze—"

"Storm, for sure," Lily insisted as the pilot cut the engine. "When you've been down here in the islands a while, you know. Okay," she added as the Hardys stood fully dressed in their gear, "over the side with you."

While Lily watched, the brothers latched two lengths of high-strength cable to their belts and fell into the water. They led the frogmen to the cargo holds. The four of them removed the first hatch, and the brothers swam through while the two frogmen moved toward the second hold.

Inside the hold, Frank looked up at the small wedge of sunlight filtering in through the hatch. Then he looked down, allowing his headlamp to illuminate the piles of crates that littered the room. They sure got knocked around a lot, Frank thought as he swam down.

Frank unraveled his length of cable and, with Joe's help, tried to tie it around one of the larger crates. This box is big enough for both of us to fit inside, Frank realized. It was extremely heavy, too—even underwater.

Frank signaled Joe that he was going to swim behind the crate. He pulled the top of the crate toward him, hoping to show Joe that he wanted him to slip the cable under the crate. Frank realized instantly that the crate would have to be tilted at a steeper angle, though.

Here goes, Frank silently grumbled, pulling at the crate. Joe must have been pushing at the same time, because instead of just lifting a few inches, the crate toppled over completely. Frank screamed silently as, in horrible underwater slow motion, the enormous crate came down on top of him, pinning him under its weight!

Chapter

10

"FRANK!" Joe forgot for an instant that he was underwater, and his shouting choked him a little. He readjusted his air regulator, then threw himself at the heavy crate, trying desperately to get it to budge. This thing must weigh a ton, Joe thought frantically, giving up on trying to lift it and working his way around to where Frank was pinned. He could see bubbles ballooning up from Frank's hose. With a sickening feeling, Joe realized that the hose had been cut. Frank had no air!

Where is everybody? Joe wished that the two frogmen hadn't gone exploring. He removed Frank's mouthpiece and replaced it with his own. Frank breathed hungrily, twitching either from pain or lack of oxygen. Joe held his breath as long as he could, then took back his mouthpiece and got a couple of quick breaths before returning it to Frank.

Joe looked up at the hatch. Still no sign of the others. He knew he couldn't free Frank without help.

Quickly calculating how long it would take him to surface, Joe removed his air tank and placed it next to his brother. Frank shook his head violently in protest. Joe took three deep breaths on the air tube, then gave the mouthpiece back to Frank and swam upward.

As he moved up through the hatch, Joe thought his lungs would explode. He finally exhaled. Just as he was about to inhale seawater, he broke the surface.

"Ahhh!" he gasped, filling his lungs with sweet air. He was on the main deck of the *Laura Baines*. The crew from the cutter were working the ship's winch to lift a huge crate from the other hold.

"Hey!" Joe said, calling to them. "My brother's trapped down there, under one of the crates! I can't get him out."

The men went into action. "We'll suit up and go down," one of the men said. Joe joined them aboard the dinghy, which they took to the cutter. Lily gave Joe a fresh air tank.

"Don't worry," she told him. "We'll get Frank back up safe and sound."

Joe and the other divers found Frank still conscious. They pried the crate off him and gently swam with him back to the deck.

By now there were several crates on the deck. The corner of one had been smashed in, and something was sticking out. Joe walked over to the crate and knelt down beside the object. "What's this?" he asked. It wasn't a weapon, and it wasn't ammunition, either.

He reached into the crate and pulled the object out. He stared at it in disbelief. "Hey!" he called out to the others. "This crate is filled with rocks!"

"Unbelievable," said one of the men. He grabbed a crowbar and pried open another crate. "Rocks!" he said at a third crate. "And more rocks! What in the world—"

"It looks," Frank observed from where he lay nursing his sore ribs, "as if somebody's already helped himself to the munitions."

Before any of them had a chance to realize what that meant, the first two divers surfaced. One of them spoke to Lily Brown. "Lieutenant," he said grimly, "we need a body bag. There's a drowned man in the hold."

Joe's breath caught in his throat. "Two of you head back to the cutter," Lily ordered the men. "Bring back a bag.

"So," Lily said, "now we have a manslaughter case. Whoever set the fire on the *Laura Baines* must be responsible for this person's death."

"How could he have drowned?" Joe asked. "Why didn't he just come up on deck when he saw the hold was flooding?"

"He was trapped down there, pinned to the water intake valve," one of the divers answered.

The other diver spoke up. "It looked as if he'd been opening it to flood the hold. The big wheel caught his arm, though, and he couldn't get free. The guy drowned himself." The diver slowly shook his head.

"Maybe he was trying to put out the fire," a man suggested.

"The fire was in hold Number Three," Lily told him. "Turning on the water there wouldn't make any difference."

While the body was being brought up, the Hardys conferred with Lily about what their findings might mean. "Rocks instead of guns," she said. "Rocks packed in grease!"

"Somebody planned the switch very carefully," Joe said. "Somebody who knew what he was doing."

"Somebody named Max Baines," Frank insisted. "He had dinner with the captain in Panama—just before the ship was sunk. And finally there was that conversation I overheard on Max's yacht. I'm convinced Max Baines and Captain Evans are in this thing together."

"None of what you've mentioned is hard evidence!" Joe protested. "You don't know that Captain Evans told Max Baines what was in his cargo hold, and you can't be sure what those people were talking about on the yacht."

"It doesn't make much difference, anyway," Lily broke in impatiently. "Whatever arms were in those crates are probably well out of the country by now."

"Maybe they were lifted off the ship after she grounded on the reef."

"No way," Frank argued. "They wouldn't have bothered to replace the contents of the crates with rocks. That was done to maintain the ship's weight, so the waterline would stay the same and nobody would notice that the guns and ammunition were missing."

"That leaves only two places where the switch could have been made," Lily said. "The Philippines, where the ship first took on her cargo, or Panama, the only other place she touched land."

"That's if you believe Captain Evans's logbook," Frank agreed.

"I believe it," Joe said stubbornly. "I don't know why I trust that guy, but I do."

"Maybe because he saved your life," Frank said. "But we still have to be objective here."

The men resurfaced with the body bag. "Transport it to the cutter," Lieutenant Brown told them. "Then come back for us, and be quick about it. A storm's coming on."

Joe looked east, where a line of black clouds

was rapidly approaching. Streaks of lightning forked along the distant horizon.

"We're in for a rough trip back," said Lily. "Look at those waves."

"You sure can predict the weather," Joe marveled. Then he spoke up about what was really on his mind. "So, Lily—if flooding the hold wouldn't put out the fire, why do you think the dead guy was opening that valve?"

"Search me," Lily said. "At first I thought he might be trying to sink the ship for insurance money, but then I remembered you two telling me that the claim had been dropped. I guess he could have been trying to cover up the theft of the arms."

The ocean swells had been high all day, but now with the approaching squall the *Laura Baines* was rocking from side to side so violently that Joe had to grab the rail to keep from falling over. "Wow," he said. "She wasn't moving like that before."

"She's a lot lighter now," Lily pointed out. "We've redistributed the weight."

At that moment Joe felt the ship's hull shift along the sand. "She's slipping!" he called out as the first raindrops fell. He glanced toward the cutter and could see the men trying to get the body bag off the dinghy. It would be several minutes before they came back.

The *Laura Baines* was now moving quite

freely with the swells. Joe heard metal twisting and saw some of the rear deck plates rip apart.

"She's breaking up!" Joe yelled as he crashed to the deck when the ship gave another violent lurch. There was a loud metallic crack, and Joe's heart leapt to his throat. The deck he was lying on was being pulled away from the rest of the ship!

"Wait for me!" Joe yelled to Lily and Frank, who had moved forward a few steps. He got to his feet, but with the next lurch of the ship, the waves came crashing over Joe's head!

Chapter

11

JOE WAS TOSSED against something hard—one of the ship's steel plates was digging into his back. Joe tried to swim for the surface, but the plate was holding him back and pulling him down.

His shirt was now caught on the edge of the steel, and he was being dragged farther under. His lungs were screaming for air, and he couldn't free himself!

This is it, Joe said to himself, trying to accept the fact that he was drowning. Just as he was about to give up, a rope appeared in front of him. Joe grabbed for it, and miraculously the rope responded, pulling him upward. Joe felt his shirt rip, and an instant later he broke the surface of the water. Raising his head, he saw

Frank and Lily hanging on to the other end of the rope.

"Atta boy, Joe!" Frank yelled over the noise of the storm. "Hang on tight!"

Seconds later Joe had rejoined the others on the deck of the *Laura Baines*—or what was left of it. He sucked in great breaths of sea air.

The rain pounded the deck and the wind whipped at their clothes as Joe, Frank, Lily, and the remaining crew members climbed into the dinghy and returned to the cutter. Soon the cutter was plowing back to San Juan, and her passengers and crew were relaxing, drinking the best fruit punch Joe had ever tasted. "You sure do appreciate food more right after you think you'll never eat again," he remarked philosophically to the group.

Joe was first through the office doors when they arrived back at the coast guard station. As the others followed, Joe greeted Major Rivera, who stood behind the counter. A dismal-looking Captain Evans stood talking with the major. "How's she doing?" Evans asked Joe, not needing to explain that he was talking about the freighter.

"She's breaking up, I'm afraid," Joe said as gently as he could. "I don't think there's any saving her now."

Two sailors carried the body bag inside, and Joe watched the major lead a shocked Evans to a back room to identify the man. When Evans returned, he seemed to be even more stunned. "It's Tim Baines, all right," he told the others. "I never thought he'd go so far as to scuttle his own dad's ship."

Tim Baines sinking the ship! Joe glanced at his brother as he remembered Tim's hints to the captain that he was involved in a special project, the map of San Xavier in Tim's cabin, and the list of Spanish-sounding names. We're closing in on someone, Joe said to himself. I just wish the guy wasn't dead.

Joe wondered briefly how any of this might tie in with the attacks on the Hardys in San Juan. He could come up with no connection for the moment, so he put the question aside.

"I just don't understand it," Captain Evans was saying, more to himself than anyone. "If Tim planned to sink the ship, why did he complain to his father about the leaks?"

"What do you mean?" the major asked.

"In Panama I overheard Tim talking to his fiancée on the telephone. He was telling her how he'd phoned his dad in the Philippines to complain about all the leaks. He said Alex had insisted the ship sail on to San Juan without repairs. I remember the conversation because I'd just sent Alex a telegram saying much the same thing."

"Did Tim say anything else?" Lily asked.

The captain frowned. "It sounded to me like the fiancée wanted Tim to switch over to his uncle Max's ship, the *Northern Star,* that was in Panama, too. Tim said he was working on some kind of project in his cabin on the *Laura Baines,* and he didn't want to move." The captain looked around the room. "I should have figured it out, I suppose. But how could I have guessed what the boy was up to?"

The door opened just then, and two young men in suits entered, closing a pair of dripping black umbrellas.

"You must be from the FBI," Major Rivera said. He explained to the others, "I contacted the agency this morning. Theft of U.S. weapons is a criminal case, out of our jurisdiction."

"That's right, sir." The agent on the left, a fresh-faced young man, flashed his ID card at the major and then replaced it in his shirt pocket. "I'm Special Agent Steve Timmerman," he said, introducing himself. "This is Special Agent Matt Reynolds."

The other agent, a red-haired young man with an intense expression, nodded self-consciously.

"You said you'd have the crew here for us to interrogate?" Agent Timmerman asked Major Rivera.

"Well, they've been hard to round up," the major said, embarrassed. "We have Captain Evans here, though. You'll want to question him."

"But the captain's innocent!" Joe protested. When no one responded—not even the captain—

Joe nudged his brother. "Come on, Frank," he said. "We have some work to do."

It was a relief to shower and change clothes on the *Sun Dancer* after the morning Joe had had. He pulled his last clean T-shirt over his last clean pair of khaki pants, painfully aware of the sunburn he'd picked up that morning on the cutter. The next day would definitely be chore day, he decided. He'd do the laundry, buy a new supply of sunscreen, swab down the deck of the *Sun Dancer,* and stock the galley with food. First, though, he and Frank had to solve this case—and rescue Captain Evans.

"Let me put it this way," he said to Frank a short time later as they devoured two lobster plates at the Club Nautico Café. "Nothing that's happened on the *Laura Baines* makes sense: The fire was useless because Alex's company forfeited its claim on the insurance; Tim's attempt to flood the hold just looks dumb, since the father he hated didn't care if the ship was destroyed."

"Yeah, but what about the stolen weapons?" Frank said, pointing with his fork at his brother. "That makes sense, if you put it together with that talk about revolutions, Max Baines, and the *Northern Star*. Add the fact that Max and the *Star* were in Panama—one of the two places the weapons might have been unloaded—

101

at the same time as the *Laura Baines,* and I'd say we're beginning to build a case."

"Exactly what I was going to say, but there's more to it than that. Remember the map of San Xavier and its capital, Santa Marta, in Tim's cabin? Put that together with the home port name, Santa Marta, painted on Max's yacht. Also San Xavier isn't far from Panama."

"Tim hated his father," Frank said, nodding thoughtfully. "It might make sense that he would team up with Max, who hated Alex, too."

"Then maybe Tim did flood the hold to cover up the arms theft," Joe said excitedly. "Maybe he got scared at the last moment that they'd be caught."

"But we're left with the same catch the captain brought up," Frank pointed out. "If he was involved in the weapons scam, why did he call his dad and demand repairs?"

Joe, stumped, chewed on his lobster. "We're close," he said stubbornly. "Of course, we still have questions. There's that one about Tim calling his dad, and then there's the mystery of why someone set fire to hold Number Three. And I also wonder if grief is really the only reason Alex Baines has stayed away."

"There's also Vince Brewer," Frank pointed out. "Is he the one who's been attacking us? If so, why—and if not, who has been? And why do Brewer and Captain Evans hate each other so much?"

Joe nodded vigorously. "Frank, it's time to go to the source for the answers."

Frank leaned forward. "You mean our prime suspect?" When Joe nodded, Frank leaned back in his chair with a satisfied smile. "There's only one person I trust to find Max Baines for us," he said. "And that's Lily Brown."

"I shouldn't tell you any of this," Lieutenant Brown whispered to the boys at the counter. "Major Rivera's just past that door, and this is a federal case now. We're supposed to be out of it completely."

"You don't have to be in it, Lily," Joe assured her. He sensed that Frank was too busy admiring how sharp Lily looked in her clean white uniform to concentrate on getting what they needed. "We're the ones who want to talk to him. You're just giving us his addresses so we won't clutter up the coast guard station anymore."

"I like having you clutter up the station," Lily said, smiling at Frank. "Before you guys showed up, my life was almost normal, believe it or not. No mysteries, no secrets, no fistfights in the halls. Here you go," she continued. "Max Baines has four homes in the U.S. alone. Plus one in Manila, one in London, one in Brazil—"

"Is there one here in San Juan?" Joe broke in.

"Sure is." Lily showed it to him so he could

103

write it down. "Just outside of town, on the coast road east of here."

"We'll find it," Frank said. He took the paper. "Just tell us where to rent a car."

The Hardys were soon breezing down the coast road, the sun shining once again on the sea to their left and the fields and lush flowers to their right.

"Turn here," Joe pointed to a dirt drive that led off the main road. "Max's place should be a mile in this direction."

Joe was relieved when they reached an iron gate embedded in two stone pillars. Beyond the gate was a security booth manned by a uniformed guard.

"Can I help you?" the guard asked in Spanish as the Hardys approached the gate.

"We'd like to speak to Mr. Baines," Frank said in English.

"And who are you?" asked the guard, also in English now.

"Frank Hardy. This is my brother, Joe. We're with the, um, Bailey-Hopgood Insurance Company."

The name didn't ring a bell with the security guard. "Mr. Baines is not here," he said. "I will tell him you called."

"When will he be back?" Joe asked.

"I can't tell you that," the guard said.

Frank thought the guard sounded amused.

"Thanks, anyway," he said, grabbing Joe by the elbow. "We'll call again next week, sir."

"Next week!" Joe protested as they left.

"Come on, Joe," Frank insisted, dragging his brother away from the gate. When they were out of earshot, he whispered, "We're not finished here."

Now that Joe understood, he got back into the car calmly. Frank backed out and drove for a quarter mile past the house. Then he pulled the car over. "Let's walk," he said. "We'll go around back and climb over the fence."

They made their way along the tall wrought-iron fence that surrounded the property. Through the fence, Joe glimpsed a luxurious Spanish-style mansion.

"Come on." Frank indicated a giant oak tree with branches hanging over the fence. Following Frank's example, Joe climbed out onto one of the branches and dropped down to the estate grounds. Ducking low, Frank and Joe moved quickly toward the house.

As the Hardys slipped behind a row of hedges only twenty yards from the pool, a telephone jangled over a loudspeaker. A maid answered the phone outside by the pool.

"Mr. Baines is in Panama, sir," Joe heard her say into the receiver. "I don't know when he will return—"

That was all Joe and Frank needed to hear.

They turned to leave but were stopped in their tracks by a dreadful growling.

Four fierce eyes shone at the Hardys from just yards away.

"Run, Joe!" Joe heard his brother scream as two dogs leapt and charged, their teeth bared. "Ruuuunn!"

Chapter

12

JOE HARDY had never run faster in his life. Gaining on him was a pair of enormous, snapping Doberman pinschers. With Frank at his side, Joe clambered up the iron fence in defiance of the laws of gravity.

He threw one leg over the top as he felt the tug of sharp teeth on his other pant cuff. The teeth were dragging him back down. He yanked his leg up, felt the fabric rip, and heard the dog fall to the ground, yelping as it made contact. Joe dropped to earth outside the estate and checked to see where Frank had landed. He raced after his brother back to the hidden car.

"Uh-oh," Frank said as they opened the car doors. "Hear that? The front gate's opening. Someone's after us. Buckle your seat belt."

Buckling himself in, too, Frank peered into his rearview mirror at the black jeep barreling toward them. Frank threw the rental car into reverse and floored the accelerator, sending the sedan hurtling backward at forty miles an hour. Honking loudly, the jeep plunged off the road to avoid being hit as Frank steered backward all the way to the coast road. Then he shifted into first and turned away from San Juan.

"If you were those guys, which way would you guess we turned—back to town or off into the country?" Frank asked.

"Gotcha," Joe said as he loosened his hold on the dashboard. "Do me a favor, Frank. Next time warn me before you do that backward thing. In fact, next time let me do the driving."

By the time they returned to San Juan it was after dark. "This place almost feels like home by now," Joe remarked as they pulled up in front of Club Nautico.

"Home never served fresh lobster three times a day," Frank pointed out, turning off the ignition. "I'm getting to like the life of a yachtsman."

The marina seemed even livelier than usual, Joe thought as he and Frank slipped into their usual places at the café. A band of musicians struck up a lively tune at the opposite end of the boardwalk as the Hardys ordered lobster again. "But broiled, this time," Joe told the waiter, "and make sure they pour on the butter."

"What's going on over there?" Frank asked after the waiter had left. A crowd had gathered around the band. They were laughing at something.

"It's an old sailor," Joe said, standing up. "He's doing a jig, trying to get the people to throw coins."

When the song ended, the sailor pushed out of the crowd and stumbled toward the café tables, insulting the diners and apparently trying to pick a fight.

"You know who he is?" Joe said with a sinking feeling in the pit of his stomach.

Frank turned. "Oh, no," he said. "Vince Brewer. And he's headed this way."

There was nowhere to hide, so the Hardys chose to grin and bear it as the former mate of the *Laura Baines* spied the brothers and swaggered toward them. He shouted in his gravelly voice, "Well, if it isn't the nosy boys!"

"Hi, Vince," Joe said. "Quite a show you put on over there."

"I do what I can," Brewer shot back as the waiter served their food. "Of course, I don't have a job on a ship anymore because everybody thinks I started a mutiny on the *Laura Baines*. You wouldn't know why they're saying that, would you?"

"What difference does it make?" Frank said, tense. "The *Laura Baines* is gone, anyway. You can't be a mate on a sunken ship."

"Right!" Brewer shouted, causing several passersby to stare. "The *Laura Baines* is a sunk ship! And I'm a sunk mate! Because *you,* wise guy," he said, pointing his finger in Joe's face, "want to testify on Monday that Captain Evans would never allow his ship to be destroyed. Well, I don't sink so easy, kid. I'd watch my back if I was you."

"You've been watching our backs for us well enough," Frank remarked. "You had us drifting on the ocean, and then there was that pleasant incident with the forklift."

Brewer seemed almost pleased by Frank's accusations. "That's right," he growled. "And there'll be more of the same if you boys don't just make up your minds to fade away."

"Mr. Brewer? Special Agent Steve Timmerman, FBI," a voice said, interrupting. "These boys may be called as witnesses in a felony case," the young, moon-faced agent recited in machine-gun fashion. "If I find you threatening them again, I'll have to arrest you on harassment charges. And by the way, no one's accusing you of anything, Brewer. So get out of here—find another job and leave these boys alone."

"But they—he—" Brewer sputtered, backing away.

"It's a federal investigation now," said Agent Reynolds from behind his partner. "You're not a suspect. Get lost."

"Thanks, guys," Joe said as Brewer hurried away. "Have a seat. Let us buy you a meal."

"We should buy you one," Agent Timmerman said eagerly, sinking into the seat facing Joe. "We just found out who you two are a few hours ago. What's it like having Fenton Hardy, best private investigator in the business, for a dad?"

"The best part," Frank quipped, "is that one of his best friends owns a truly magnificent sailboat."

"Seriously," Agent Reynolds cut in, taking a seat between his partner and Joe, "we studied some of your father's cases at the academy. We're real fans. We heard you guys do some detecting, too."

"Now and then," Joe said with a grin. "Speaking of which, why'd you tell Vince Brewer he was off the hook? Is the maritime court inquiry really canceled?"

"As far as we know," Agent Reynolds replied. "Once you get illegal arms involved, it becomes pretty clear that small-fry like Brewer can't possibly be involved. Have you ever tried to talk to that guy? He's dumb as a post. We have our eyes on Captain Evans at the moment. He's hiding something. But keep that under your hats."

"What about Max Baines?" Frank asked as he signaled the waiter for menus for the agents.

"Baines?" Agent Timmerman said. "He's in the Philippines, from what I understand. We're working to get him back here for questioning."

"No, that's Alex Baines," Joe explained patiently, reminding himself that the two agents had just been assigned to the case. "Max is his brother. Max owns a rival shipping company, and the brothers are bitter enemies. We have reason to believe Max might be behind the arms sales."

"What evidence?" Agent Reynolds asked sharply.

"We overheard a couple of members of the crew of his yacht talking about revolution," Frank explained. "And Alex's son, Tim, was Max's ally. It was Tim who tried to flood the ship. We think Max might have stolen the weapons from the hold and sold them without his brother's knowledge."

"Impossible," Reynolds observed. "How could he unload the cargo without the crew knowing? One of them would have come forward by now. They all want to get this behind them and get on with their lives."

"Right. It's Evans, or else it's Alex Baines," Timmerman agreed, scanning the menu. "This Max guy doesn't even sound close."

"Wait a minute, though," Reynolds said, snapping his fingers. "I saw Max Baines's name on the marina records when I was checking them this afternoon. His yacht was moored here, right?"

"Right," said Joe. "A beauty named *Megabucks*."

Timmerman nodded. "I remember. It was

headed for Panama, according to the records. What a life those guys lead, eh?"

After the Hardys and the agents had eaten, Joe and Frank returned to the *Sun Dancer* to get some sleep. "I can't wait to tell Dad that FBI recruits study his moves now," Joe said with a chuckle. "Those agents aren't the brightest."

"They sure didn't want to hear anything against Max Baines," Frank agreed. "But don't underestimate them, Joe. Maybe they suspect Baines and don't want us to know."

"Or maybe," Joe added flippantly, "he's too rich and important for them to consider as a suspect. One thing's for sure, though—Vince Brewer will stay away from us now."

"Now that I've seen how pathetic he is, I'm not even mad at him anymore," Frank replied. "I even hope he finds another job."

"Speaking of jobs," Joe said, "are you thinking what I'm thinking—that a trip to Panama is in order?"

"Well, let's see. We think that's where the arms transfer took place," Frank said with mock seriousness. "We know Max is there. We just found out that the *Megabucks* is on its way. It's only a two-hour flight from here, and because the court inquiry's been canceled, we no longer have to stay put."

"Let's get some shut-eye," Joe said. "We have plenty to do in the morning."

* * *

By noon the next day the Hardys had bought plane tickets, flown to Panama City, rented a red convertible at the airport, and were driving along the highway to Santo Cristo Hospital, where Captain Evans had told them he'd spent the two days that were missing from his log.

"I can't get over how different this city looks from San Juan," Joe said, taking in the squat, drab buildings.

"I want to get back to San Juan as soon as possible," Frank said. "Now that we're free to deliver the *Sun Dancer* to Florida, we ought to do it. But first we check out Evans's story at the hospital. If he wasn't sick, he has some explaining to do when we get back. If he was, maybe his doctor can tell us more about how it happened."

"I can think of more fun things to do than discuss Captain Evans's digestive system," said Joe.

Frank steered toward a six-story hospital with a large sign reading Santo Cristo in front. "After this we'll find the *Megabucks*."

The hospital receptionist referred Joe and Frank to a Dr. Gomez, a well-built man with glasses and a mustache whom the Hardys found in the hospital lab. "Yes, Captain Daniel Evans was here—for two days, I think," Gomez told them, going over Captain Evans's chart as two nurses analyzed blood samples a short distance behind him. "Salmonella poisoning. Yes, he was quite sick for a day or so. Salmonella is quite common in the tropics." The doctor closed the chart. "Anything else I can help you with?"

"Could I have a look at the chart?" Frank asked. "Just to verify the exact dates?"

The doctor hesitated. Frank could see he didn't want to comply. Just then, one of the nurses leaned against a tray of blood samples and accidentally sent it crashing to the floor. Gomez ran to help the nurses, leaving the chart on the table.

Frank leaned over and flipped through the captain's file while Joe tried to block Gomez's view. Just as Frank was closing the chart, Dr. Gomez looked up and caught Frank in the act.

"Will that be all?" Gomez asked icily.

"Yes, sir," Frank replied. "Thank you."

Frank led his brother to the elevator. "Gomez lied about the captain," Frank muttered to Joe as the elevator doors closed behind them. "Salmonella didn't poison Captain Evans. Arsenic did."

"Arsenic?" Joe demanded as Frank punched a button on the elevator and it stopped at the next floor. "You mean, somebody tried to kill him?"

"They found just a small trace—enough to make him sick. But why did Gomez lie about it—to us and to the captain? Who's he trying to protect?"

Frank ushered Joe out of the elevator. "We're

going back upstairs," he explained to Joe. "I want to see what the doctor's doing now. My guess is he's furious that I got a look at that file."

The brothers returned to the laboratory, but the doctor wasn't there. Following the nurses' directions to his office, the Hardys heard Gomez's voice on the telephone, loud enough to carry through the closed door. He was speaking English. "You told me there would be no problem," he was complaining. "I know, but the payoff wasn't big enough to risk my reputation, my whole life's work!"

Frank put his ear to the door and heard the doctor say, "Just get these guys off my back, okay?" Frank heard the phone being slammed down into its cradle and footsteps moving toward the door. "Let's beat it!" he whispered to Joe.

Joe backed up and stumbled into a gurney. The gurney went sliding out from behind him, and Joe fell backward onto the floor. Dr. Gomez's door flew open and the doctor stared at them, openmouthed. "You!" he shouted, murder in his eyes.

Frank and Joe raced down the hall with the enraged doctor in hot pursuit. "Split up!" Frank said. Nodding, Joe went one way down the corridor, and Frank went the other.

Hearing footsteps coming after him, Frank felt pleased. At least Joe will get away, he thought.

Rounding a corner, Frank ducked through an open door and closed it behind him.

It's so quiet in here, Frank thought as he stood with his weight against the closed door. When he'd caught his breath, he moved forward into the dimly lit room. He bumped into a long, narrow table. Frank gasped. On the table was a human corpse!

He backed away from the dissecting cleaver that lay next to the body. Then he noticed the large, deep drawers in one wall that had to contain other dead bodies. "Wow," Frank whispered out loud. "A real morgue!"

Hearing footsteps approaching, Frank thought fast. He pulled open drawer after drawer, looking for an empty one. Finally he found one and slipped inside, pulling it closed most of the way just as Dr. Gomez entered the room.

Frank peered through the small opening, hoping the doctor would leave. The doctor's gaze passed over the drawers on the wall, including the drawer where Frank was hiding. Did he see me? Frank wondered.

He didn't have long to wonder. Dr. Gomez approached the table in the center of the room. He picked up the dissecting cleaver. Then, with a menacing grin, he turned toward Frank.

Chapter

13

JOE HALF RAN, HALF SLID down the well-waxed corridors, brushing past surprised orderlies, nurses, and patients. He raced down the stairs all the way to the first floor before it struck him that Dr. Gomez wasn't following him. He's following Frank, Joe realized, and instantly turned to retrace his steps. He couldn't let Frank fight that creep alone.

Starting his search outside Gomez's office, Joe methodically checked each room in the direction Frank had gone. He opened the first door off a new corridor and found, in the center of the room, Dr. Gomez, his back to Joe.

Instinctively, Joe froze in place, watching as Gomez put down a dissecting tool he had in his hand and picked up a large syringe. This is the morgue! Joe realized, noticing the cadaver for the first time. He saw Gomez approach the drawers in the far wall, brandishing the syringe. It didn't take much for Joe to realize Frank was hiding in one of them.

Joe waited until Gomez had reached the drawer. Then he yelled, "Hey, you!" As Gomez turned, the drawer flew open, slamming into the doctor's back. Before Gomez could recover, Joe was on him and had knocked the doctor out with a well-placed karate chop to the neck.

"We'd better keep you out of the way for a while," Frank said. He dragged the doctor over to the drawer he had left and lifted him inside. "There," he said, closing it. "That ought to hold you for half an hour or so."

"Good going, Frank," Joe said as the two of them left the hospital and walked out into the warm Panamanian sun. "Where do we find Max Baines?"

"On his yacht, of course," Frank said. "Where else?"

The brothers headed for Panama City's bustling port. Joe couldn't stop trying to stare in all directions at once—at the women in bright-colored clothes selling fruit and handicrafts, at the variety of boats moored in the harbor, and at the tropical trees and flowers that grew everywhere in unorderly abandon.

Frank hardly noticed his surroundings as he parked the car and hurried toward the harbormaster's office. When Joe caught up, Frank was asking the portly, middle-aged man whether the *Megabucks* was docked there.

"No, senors," the man told the Hardys. "The owner, Mr. Baines, was here recently for two days, on his freighter, the *Northern Star*. But on his yacht, no."

"I guess he hasn't gotten here yet," Joe said. "He'll be here tomorrow by the latest."

Frank eyed the harbormaster warily. "Thank you, sir," he said. "Adios." Pulling Joe out of the office, Frank whispered to him as soon as they were alone, "Max Baines is here all right. His housekeeper said so, remember?"

"Yeah, but maybe he's just not here yet," Joe argued.

"If our theory is correct about his stealing the munitions here, that means this is his center of operations—this is where he sells arms and gets paid for them," Frank continued.

"So you think he's here to meet a client?" Joe asked.

"Maybe. Or to get paid for that last shipment."

"But who is he selling the weapons to?"

Frank shook his head. "I keep thinking about how they used the word *revolución* on the *Megabucks*. Maybe there's going to be a revolution or a military coup around here."

"Wow!" Joe said. " 'The Hardys Save Panama!' I can see the headlines now."

"Get serious, will you?" Frank said, frowning. "First of all, I don't necessarily mean Panama. Secondly, I think that harbormaster knows more than he's saying. Now, we're going back in there to find out what it is, okay?"

This time, Frank took a different tack when he entered the harbormaster's office. "Senor, sorry to bother you again," he began, "but there is one more thing we'd like to ask you." The man nodded and Frank went on. "When Mr. Baines was here on the *Northern Star,* was the freighter docked here in the harbor?"

"No, senor. It was waiting out at sea for permission to pass through the canal."

"Were there any other ships waiting to pass through besides that one?" Frank asked.

The harbormaster was confused. "I will check my register," he said. He pulled a thick book from behind his desk and leafed through it. "Only one," he said. "The name was the *Laura Baines.*"

"The *Laura Baines!* I see." Frank glanced at his brother. So, Frank said to himself. The harbormaster may have been bribed not to tell anyone Max Baines was in town, but no one paid him to be quiet about a run-down freighter called the *Laura Baines!*

"Do you know if the two ships exchanged any cargo?" he asked.

"I could not see the ships, senor," the harbormaster said pleasantly enough.

"Where is the *Northern Star* now?" Joe broke in.

The man's eyes clouded over again. "Her destination was registered as Lisbon. She may already be there. Who knows?"

'Hmmm." Frank rubbed his chin. "Thank you, senor. Adios again."

This time, when the two brothers left the office, the harbormaster did not wave goodbye.

"Now what?" Joe asked. "Do we search the harbor for Max's yacht?"

"All we can do is keep an eye out for her," Frank said. "We should also check in at the pilot's station and try to find the guy who piloted the *Northern Star* into the canal."

Ten minutes later Joe found himself shaking hands with a grizzled old seaman named Captain Esteban. Frank said Esteban was the pilot who had handled the *Northern Star*. To Joe's relief, the captain had a pretty good command of English. At least, Joe thought, it was better than Frank's Spanish.

"Sí." The captain nodded when they asked him whether he'd seen anything interesting. *"Sí, I notice."* He said nothing more, but just kept nodding and grinning. Joe pulled out his wallet and handed Esteban a twenty-dollar bill.

"Very interesting thing I see," said the captain, like a music box someone had just wound up. "Boxes. Many boxes. Big ones. They take boxes at night, before the sun comes. I was not sleeping. I am old, my back is not so good. I was not asleep. I see everything."

"You didn't call the police?" Joe asked.

"The police?" Esteban looked at Joe with pity. "Why? So I can be arrested for not minding the business of Captain Esteban, but instead I am minding the business of some general? I see the uniforms on the boats. I am not saying anything. You, you are Americanos. You do not understand Panama. Here it is different."

"Thank you, Captain," Frank said. He nodded to Joe, who grudgingly slapped another twenty-dollar bill into the man's trembling hand.

"Give me a fifty," Frank whispered to Joe.

Joe stared at his brother, not moving.

"A fifty. It's important."

Shaking his head, Joe handed over a fifty-dollar bill from his wallet. Frank held the bill up where the captain could see it. Then he said, "Captain, is there anything else you can tell us about the *Northern Star?*"

"*Sí*, senor," the captain said. "I can tell you something very good. The *Northern Star*, she has trouble in the engine. She is still here."

Joe's eyes widened. "In Panama City?"

"No, senor. In Colón. At the other end of the canal." Esteban snatched the fifty from Frank. As the Hardys jumped up the captain added, "You are very lucky hombres!"

Frank and Joe dashed for the car. "How many

hours to Colón from here?" Joe called out as he opened the door and slid into the driver's seat.

Frank got in the car and answered, "Who knows? The sooner we get started, the sooner we get there."

It was the afternoon rush hour, and that meant the roads were clogged with big American cars from the fifties and sixties, belching exhaust fumes into the extremely hot air.

At the corner ahead, a police officer held up his hand to stop the traffic. Joe braked the car.

On the passenger side, Frank glanced out the open window. As he did so, a black limousine with closed windows pulled up alongside them. As Frank gazed at the tinted glass, seeing himself in the reflection, the window glided down.

Behind the glass was the barrel of an enormous gun. It was pointed right at Frank's head.

"Joe—duck!" Frank screamed as the gun exploded in his face.

Chapter

14

FRANK FELT the bullet whistle through his hair. He heard Joe yell, "Frank! Are you okay?" as he hit the accelerator. The car sped forward with a jerk.

Behind them, Frank heard the gun fire again. He turned to see the traffic officer diving out of the way as the limousine sped past him. Meanwhile, Joe slammed on the brakes just in time to avoid hitting a parked car at the side of the road. The car died and wouldn't start again.

"I'm fine," Frank said dryly. "But we've got trouble."

The doors to the limousine had opened, and three men with rifles were getting out. "Let's go," Frank ordered.

"Around this corner!" Frank shouted. As

they ducked around the corner, Frank spotted a large hotel halfway down the block with international flags flying over the front doors. "In there!" he called out.

Running up the steps of the hotel, Frank saw the three armed men rounding the corner. One of them saw Frank and Joe and shouted to his pals. The brothers ducked into the hotel lobby. "Now where?" Joe asked.

"Over there." Frank pointed to the dining room of the hotel's restaurant. They ran through the dining room into the kitchen. Looking back through the glass oval in the door, Frank saw their pursuers enter the dining room. Patrons screamed and ducked for cover at the sight of the rifles.

"*Salida!*" Frank screamed at the cook. "*Salida!* Where's the exit?"

"Over there," the man said in English, pointing to a flight of stairs leading downward. "Through the cellar and out the back."

As Frank and Joe ran to the stairs, a shot rang out behind them, and plaster splintered on the wall next to Joe's head.

"Whoa!" Joe gasped as they ducked into an alley. "Here, let's hide behind these trash cans till we catch our breath."

As they crouched there, they saw the three men run past them down the alley. At a corner, they hesitated before splitting up in three directions. "Now's our chance," Frank said. "Let's get out of here."

"Hey, Frank," Joe said, jogging beside his brother. "What are we going to do?"

"Look, Joe," Frank said. "There's a train station."

"Do you suppose we could get to Colón that way?" Joe asked.

"It's worth a try," Frank replied.

Carefully they made their way across the busy avenue to the train station. The station was swarming with armed men in uniform, but none of them appeared to be on alert. Frank bought two second-class tickets to Colón on a train leaving in ten minutes. The ticket agent told him there were no first-class seats on that particular train.

The Hardys spent ten minutes making themselves inconspicuous. Then they boarded the train with the rest of the crowd and took their seats.

"Do you think anyone saw us get on?" Joe asked as they tried to make themselves comfortable. Frank was surprised to see a pair of chickens wander past their seats.

"I hope not," Frank said, smiling politely at the very large family crammed with their rooster into the seats across from the Hardys. "At least we're out of there. Whew." He shook his head.

Joe sniffed. "This train smells weird," he

said. "Oh, well. Colón's not that far. How long a trip can it be?"

Very long, the boys soon realized. The train stopped at every tiny station along the way to let off and take on people and animals.

"This will not go down as one of my favorite days," Joe remarked miserably.

Gradually, Frank noticed, the terrain grew more overgrown, until it seemed they were traveling through dense jungle. There were fewer stops now, and at one of them the family with the rooster finally disembarked.

Soon it grew dark, and the train crept slowly through the blackness lit only by the full moon. Frank's eyes closed wearily, then opened again, and finally closed again. The next thing he knew, Joe was shaking him awake.

"Frank!" he said. "Look at all those lights up ahead."

The sign at the station read, Gamboa. As far as Frank could tell, the station belonged to a tiny village surrounded by jungle. But it was lit by several searchlights, and there were men in uniforms everywhere, all of them with guns. The train screeched to a stop, and two of the men got on board several cars ahead of the Hardys. The train pulled out of the station.

"You don't think they're looking for us, do you?" Joe asked doubtfully.

"Us?" Frank frowned. "Why? You think

they're friends with the guys who were shooting at us?"

"It's possible," Joe said. "Those guys might have called ahead and told them to intercept us. You're the one who said Max Baines probably has a lot of paid friends."

"True," Frank agreed as the door at the far end of the car opened and two men entered. Frank studied them. It was impossible for outsiders like Frank and Joe to tell by the uniforms whether they were police, soldiers, or revolutionaries. "It doesn't seem very likely—I doubt that Max or his clients think we're worth that much trouble. On the other hand, I'd hate to be wrong."

"You've convinced me," Joe said in a low voice as the men moved slowly down the aisle. The other passengers in the hot, cramped car were fumbling for identity papers and engaging the men in long conversations. "Let's go," Joe murmured. He and Frank stood up and, turning their backs to the two men, started walking away.

"Atención! Señores!" Frank heard behind them. *"Atención!"*

"They're after us, Joe. Run!" Frank ordered. Together, they scrambled through the car door and shut it behind them. The police ran after them, struggling to open the rusty old doors.

Frank and Joe ran through several cars, sending chickens and children shrieking, until Frank realized there was only one more car to go. "In here," he said, opening a washroom door. He and Joe crammed inside, shutting the door behind them. They heard footsteps run past.

"Now what?" Joe asked, looking out the small window into the night. "They'll be back any second. There's nowhere else to run."

"Nowhere but the jungle," Frank said.

"Are you kidding?" Joe said. "Who do you think we are—Tarzan and Cheeta? What do we know about finding our way through the jungle?"

"I'll tell you one thing," said Frank, hearing the footsteps approach again. "Under the circumstances, I'm willing to learn."

"Atención! Señores!" called one officer, banging on the door with his fist.

"Now!" Frank shouted, kicking out the window. Frank went out the small window feet first, landing in the underbrush and rolling. Joe landed seconds after he did. The train took off then and moved slowly into the dark night.

"Hey," Joe said brightly. "We can just walk down the tracks all the way to Colón!"

"If those guys weren't after us before, the way we acted just now sure drew their attention to us. They might have someone check along the tracks for us. Maybe we can find a road that goes along the tracks. Then we can hug the trees near it."

By the light of the full moon, Frank picked a likely direction and plunged into the underbrush beside the tracks. Soon the brothers were sur- rounded by pitch darkness, and found them- selves knee-deep in warm, swampy water. All around insects and night animals called. The air was muggy, and Frank felt as though he were swimming.

"Great. Just great," Frank said. "Well, if there is a road it sure isn't on this side of the railroad tracks. It's so wet in here I feel like we've walked straight into the canal."

"Okay, so we guessed wrong," Joe said reso- lutely. "All we have to do is—"

He stopped in midsentence. "Frank," he said, "do you see what I see?"

"I don't see anything," Frank grumbled, mov- ing closer to Joe.

"Watch carefully," Joe said, not moving. "There's a lump in that pool of light up ahead. And it's alive."

In silence the brothers peered at the lump. It changed to a long, dark shape and slipped into the water, making hardly a ripple.

"Joe!" he said in an urgent whisper. "Run for it! It's a crocodile!"

Chapter

15

JOE FROZE, unable to move in the frightening darkness. He heard several other soft splashes, and glimpsed two other moonlit ripples moving toward him.

"The tree, Joe!" Frank shouted, sloshing toward him. "Over your head!"

Joe looked up. Over his head, barely visible, was the low-slung limb of a banyan tree. Joe leapt for it. His fingers brushed the limb but couldn't grasp it. The ripples came steadily closer.

Now Frank was there, lifting him. Joe grabbed hard and swung himself up and over with all his might. "Frank, grab on!" he yelled, reaching down. Frank grabbed his brother, and Joe pulled so hard that he nearly fell off the limb backward.

As Frank swung his legs up, open jaws rose out of the water and snapped shut, just missing Frank.

"They must be hungry," Frank said, gaining a better position on the limb. "We'd better get out of here before they call for reinforcements."

Taking a cue from his brother, Joe shimmied down the length of the limb to a spot where it hung over dry land. There, he dropped to the ground and waited for Frank to do the same. The angry crocodiles began swimming back toward them. "Let's not stick around," Frank suggested, taking off at a steady run.

A moment later Joe stood on the railroad tracks again. "Look," he said to Frank, pointing down the line to the flash of distant flashlights on the railbed. "They must have stopped the train again to look for us."

"Let's go this way, then," Frank said, crossing to the other side of the tracks.

This time the brothers soon found a road. "Paved and everything," Joe remarked, tapping his shoe on its surface. "Well, brother? To Colón?"

"After you," said Frank.

It was nearly dawn before the first vehicle passed the Hardys. "Look," said Frank, eyeing the cargo. "Some farmer's taking his chickens to market."

Without even consulting Joe, Frank hailed the

driver and asked to pay for a ride into Colón. Moments later the boys were making themselves comfortable among the cages in the back.

"We're going to smell lovely after this," Joe said sleepily, covering himself with straw.

"I don't like it any better than you do," Frank retorted, "but it beats getting eaten by crocodiles."

When the Hardys woke, they found themselves in a bustling, attractive port city. As he and Frank said goodbye to the farmer and made their way to the port, Joe found himself excited at being in a new place. Joe had always been fascinated by the awesome idea of a canal cut between two oceans. Now he'd have a chance to see the Panama Canal firsthand.

Frank checked in with the harbormaster at the port and was told that the *Northern Star* was anchored at the far end of the docks. As the Hardys walked down the street parallel to the docks, they were forced to make way for a long, white limousine to pass. "Could it be?" Frank said, starting to trot after the slow-moving car. Joe jogged after him.

The limousine pulled up at the last wharf, where the *Northern Star* was berthed. The Hardys watched as Max Baines emerged from the car. The shipowner walked briskly to board his ship. The limousine pulled back into traffic and soon disappeared.

"What I'd give to get on that ship," Frank said hotly.

"You know that the weapons may already be gone," Joe suggested.

"I don't believe it." Frank shook his head. "He hasn't had them that long, and this kind of business takes time."

As if in answer to the boys' questions, a black limousine pulled up at the wharf. From out of the backseat emerged three men in uniforms who walked quickly toward the gangway. Their limousine remained where it was.

"Hey, Joe," Frank said excitedly, "those are the three guys I saw through the binoculars at the marina in San Juan—the ones who gave Max Baines the envelope!"

"You think this might be the big payoff?" Joe asked, eyeing the men as they boarded the ship.

"Could be," Frank said, nodding.

"We've got to get aboard that ship!"

"We will," Frank assured him. "But it's safer to wait till after dark."

"But—"

"Don't worry, Joe. As I said, chances are if this is the payoff, the weapons still haven't been unloaded. And they're not going to unload them in broad daylight. Come on, let's go pay a visit to a public bath. I'm sick of smelling like a chicken."

* * *

As soon as it got dark, the Hardys made their way back to the wharf where the *Northern Star* was berthed. Peering down the wharf to the gangway, Frank was not surprised to see two armed guards sitting and enjoying the balmy night air.

"How are we going to get on board now?" Joe asked.

Frank nodded to the mooring ropes. "Think we can shimmy up those?"

Joe cracked a smile. "Hey, all we have to do is imagine crocodiles snapping at our heels," he said.

"Good idea," Frank agreed. "But do you think we can do it without those guys noticing us?"

Joe glanced at the guards ogling a couple of pretty girls walking by.

"Looks like they're more interested in other things," Joe said. "Let's give it a try."

Sneaking onto the wharf, hugging the bulkheads for cover, the brothers reached the mooring ropes. Joe waited until Frank had shimmied on board unnoticed, then took his turn. "Success!" he whispered to Frank as he hoisted himself over the rail and onto the deck. "Now what?"

"There are lights on in the saloon area," Frank said, "and one of the portholes is open. Let's go listen." He crept over to the porthole, motioning for Joe to follow.

The men inside were speaking English, Joe

noted gratefully. "Mr. Baines," a voice said, "our movement is very grateful to you. When our mission is completed, you will, of course, have a status in our country of the most privileged order."

"I should hope so," said a grumpy-sounding Max Baines. "After all I've gone through to get this stuff for you. Now, you're sure your men know what to do with it?"

"*Sí,* Senor Baines. My men will be waiting at the beach to unload the cargo. The coup will take place as soon as the weapons are assembled. The time of the attack is scheduled for sunrise. Our island is not large, senor, as you know. The president's house is guarded by only one small regiment. The weapons you have brought us will be more than enough. Afterward, we three will be in complete control. Democracy, Senor, is bad for business, but when we are in charge, business, for you especially, will be very good. San Xavier can be a very friendly place."

Joe looked at Frank, wide-eyed. "San Xavier, Frank! That's where the coup will be!"

Frank nodded. It was the island where Max Baines's yacht was registered. The island whose map Tim Baines had been studying the day he died. Of course—Frank felt dumb for not having realized it before—San Xavier must be where the revolutionaries come from.

"What do we do?" he heard Joe whisper.

Frank thought quickly. If they tried to alert the Panamanian officials, there was no guarantee they would take any action to stop the coup. The Americans in the Canal Zone? Maybe they could—

The noise of the ship's engine revving up, and the sound of running footsteps, put an end to Frank's speculations. "She's getting under way!" Joe gasped.

"We're going with her, Joe," Frank said under his breath. "We'd better hide."

Joe dashed over to a small motorboat covered with canvas. "In here," he said, lifting the canvas. The boys pulled the canvas over themselves.

Frank could hear the ship coming to life as they headed out of the harbor. After two or three hours, the ship's engines went quiet, and Frank heard the anchor chain dropping. "We must be there already," Frank whispered. "Any ideas on how to stop this thing from happening?"

"We'll think of something," Joe whispered back.

Then Frank heard Max Baines's voice. "I'm going to the barge. Captain, have your men lower a boat for us. Have the crates ready for loading when we return with the barge."

"Aye, aye, Mr. Baines," came the gruff captain's voice. Then the man shouted to the crew,

"Lower boat Number One. Have her ready in five minutes. Mr. Baines doesn't like to be kept waiting."

Frank tensed, his senses quick, his heart racing. "Boat number one," he repeated. "Joe—that's our boat!"

Chapter

16

"JONES," the captain ordered, "you go untie her. You other men open the hatches and get busy unloading. That barge will be here within the hour."

As one sailor approached their boat, Joe lifted the corner of the canvas ever so slightly to see his target. Checking to make sure Frank was ready, Joe threw back the entire canvas. "Hi there!" he said.

Before the surprised sailor could raise an alarm, Frank landed a punch and the man fell limp to the deck.

"Okay. Now, put him in there." Joe pointed to one of the large funnels that provided ventilation for the lower depths of the ship. Frank and

Joe hoisted the unconscious sailor into the funnel, then scrambled in with him, just in time to avoid being seen by the crew.

"Wow! It's hot in here!" Joe heard Frank whisper.

"We're right above the ship's boilers," Joe said, wiping his forehead with his shirt-sleeve.

"Whew," Frank said. "I feel like I'm going to pass out."

"Look, Frank," Joe said, peeking out the top of the funnel. "They're lowering Baines and the rebels in the boat."

"Somehow, we have to foil their plans."

"The ship's radio?" Joe suggested. "We could call for help."

"There you go," Frank said, nodding. "We're still within two hundred miles of the Canal Zone, and it's still U.S. territory. That means the coast guard could send help."

"If we can reach them," Joe said. "Let's give it a try."

They crept out of the funnel and along the deck until they came to the ladder leading up to the bridge. Above them, Joe could see the back of a crewman holding a rifle. "I'll tackle him," Joe told his brother.

Climbing catlike up the ladder, Joe threw himself at the unsuspecting guard. The man tumbled forward with a grunt, but as he hit the bridge rail, his gun went off with a loud bang and fell into the ocean. By the time Joe had dispatched the guard with a right hook to the jaw, the entire crew was rushing back along the lower deck. "They must have thought the shot came from the cabins below," Joe cried.

"That gives us a minute or so at most," Frank agreed. "Can you hold them off while I radio for help?"

Joe grabbed a fire extinguisher off its brackets. "I can try," he said grimly. He braced himself against the wheelhouse door, while Frank went in search of the radio room.

Frank had just disappeared from view when the first crew members spotted Joe. Calling to their mates, they started toward him. As they began climbing the ladder, Joe brought the extinguisher out from behind him and let them have it with a blast of chemical spray. Okay, he said to himself, this is great—as long as the extinguisher holds out.

It didn't take long for Frank to find the radio room. Fortunately, it was empty. Frank slipped inside and sent out a call for help, including the *Northern Star*'s location and a brief description of what was happening on board.

Just as he finished transmitting his message, though, everything went black—the lights, the radio, everything. Had anyone received his message? Could they get there in time? Frank had no way of knowing. All he knew for now was that he had better help Joe!

Frank searched the drawers and cabinets in the radio room, looking for ideas. "Come on," he muttered nervously, "there has to be something."

Finally in a cabinet in the far corner, he found a bottle of vodka. "Yes!" Frank cried, grabbing the bottle and twisting off the cap in one movement. He ripped off the tail of his shirt and doused it with the vodka. Then he stuffed the cloth down inside the neck of the bottle.

Time to go, Frank urged himself nervously. He grabbed a book of matches from one of the drawers and quickly moved toward the bridge.

There was the crew, bunched together and by the moon. Two of them had rifles and were taking occasional potshots at Joe. Frank spotted Joe ducked behind a bulkhead, darting out to spray chemicals at the crew whenever the shooting stopped.

As one of the crew took aim at Joe, Frank struck a match, lit the end of the shirttail that was sticking out of the bottle, and tossed it toward the crew. The burning bottle landed on the deck and exploded in a shower of glass shards and flaming bits of cloth. As eerie blue flames flew everywhere, the crew scattered in panic. They don't know how many intruders are on the ship, Frank realized. He needed to keep them guessing as long as possible.

Frank grabbed a ring life preserver hanging nearby and sent it sailing toward a crew member like a Frisbee. The sailor jumped backward, looking around wildly. Satisfied, Frank turned and ran back to join his brother.

"About time you showed up," Joe remarked to his brother. "I'm just about out of spray. Did you reach the coast guard?"

"I'm not sure. Somebody shut down the power before I received an answer."

A shot rang out, interrupting him. "Uh-oh," Joe said. "I think they're figuring out we're the only ones aboard."

"That was bound to happen sooner or later," Frank said. In his head, he was calculating how long the coast guard would take to arrive. An hour at the soonest, he figured, even with the fastest cutter they had, and even if it was ready to go at a moment's notice. "We'd better think of something else to keep these guys busy."

Before Joe could answer, Frank heard a loud cry from above. Two crewmen were dropping down on them from the roof of the wheelhouse! One of them—a swarthy, heavyset sailor—landed on top of Frank. As he struggled to free himself, Frank caught sight of more crew members ready to descend.

"Joe!" Frank gasped as the sailor landed a punch. "Run!"

Frank was unable to say more. The sailor's

hands had closed around his neck in an iron grip. The sailor shook Frank as he choked him, and the world started to spin and blur. He's killing me, Frank thought vaguely, ceasing to struggle. I'm going to die and never know how this case ends!

Chapter

17

"Aaaugh!" Frank sputtered as the sailor choked the last air from his lungs. Then, as in a dream, Frank heard the captain's voice command, "Ease off, men. Mr. Baines will want to question them before we finish them off."

The iron grip relaxed, and Frank sucked in a huge gulp of air. Beside him, Joe was pinned to the deck by four sailors.

Frank heard the sound of a motor approaching on the ocean. "That'll be the barge," the captain said. "Some of you go throw her a line. Don't worry about these two," he added, drawing a pistol. "They aren't going anywhere."

Frank exchanged a glance with Joe as Max Baines himself appeared at the top of the ladder a few minutes later. He walked over to the boys, shaking his head sadly.

"I thought we took care of these two in Panama," he said to the captain. "Evidently, they're more resourceful than we thought." He knelt down between Frank and Joe and said, "You've been a nuisance, boys—sticking your noses in where they don't belong. But I'll make you a deal: Tell me who sent you down here and what they know about this, and I'll allow you to die quickly and painlessly. Otherwise . . ." He shrugged. "It's up to you."

Frank glanced at his brother, then back at the tanned face of the shipowner. "We're the only ones on the case, Mr. Baines," Frank told him. "Nobody even knows we're here."

"Oh, come now." Max chuckled humorlessly. "You don't expect me to believe that."

Behind them, Frank could hear the winch cranking up to transfer the deadly cargo from the ship to the barge. "Mr. Baines," Frank said, "if you wanted to steal weapons, why didn't you have the government put them on one of your ships?"

"Since you're going to die very shortly, I guess it won't hurt to explain it to you. My brother, Alex, and I are enemies, you see. You know, he won't even be able to collect the insurance money on the ship I sank!" Baines laughed, his smooth skin glistening in the moonlight.

"That's why you canceled the insurance claim for Alex?" Joe said, amazed. "To cheat him?"

"It was a hard choice," Baines admitted, "whether to frame Alex in an insurance scam or make sure he lost a million dollars. When Alex refused to return to San Juan, I decided it was taking too long to wait for him to be arrested. So I canceled the insurance claim instead."

"What a guy," Joe muttered.

Baines glared at him, but then his face relaxed. "I had my reasons," he said. "Alex's contract with the army was very lucrative. The army had rejected my own very reasonable bid, and that angered me, of course.

"Now, at the same time, some friends of mine in San Xavier had been planning a little revolution. They promised me some excellent future business deals if only I'd help them come up with some weapons. So I hatched a plan to kill two birds with one stone—so to speak."

Joe glared at Baines. "At least one man is dead because of you," he said. "Your own nephew!"

"Yes, poor Tim," Max said. "He was the only person on earth who despised his father as much as I did. I'll miss him."

Frank noted that Baines didn't look grief-stricken. "How did the plan work?" he asked Baines, stalling for time.

Baines warmed to his subject. "We gave Captain Evans a dose of arsenic in Panama City."

"We know," Joe said. "And paid a doctor to lie about it."

"Right," Frank chimed in. "So while Evans was in the hospital you made the switch—offshore, in the middle of the night, when you thought no one could see you."

"Tim made sure most of the crew of the *Laura Baines* spent that night on shore leave," Baines agreed cheerfully. "The others he drugged. We lifted tons of munitions from the hold of that lard bucket, and no one was ever the wiser. I even had the brilliant idea to make Tim pretend to demand repairs on the ship from his father, so that Alex would be on record for refusing to do so."

"Why should he have repaired it?" Joe said angrily. "He knew it was going to be scrapped the minute it returned to San Juan!"

"Yes, he wasn't faring very well, business-wise," Baines admitted. "Over the last years, I've managed to run him right into the ground."

"Then what happened aboard the *Laura Baines?*" Joe asked. "I guess Vince Brewer must have kept you informed."

"What do you mean?" Baines said, surprised. "I'd never trust a stupid thug like him."

"He tried to kill us—twice," Joe told him.

"I'm not surprised," Baines retorted. "I'm told he panicked when he saw the fire and ordered the men to abandon ship. That was the idea—set the fire to get the men off the boat, lock up that crazy captain, smash the radio equipment, then have Tim sink her, hopping into the last boat to get away."

"So Brewer just wanted us out of the way so we wouldn't testify against him?" Joe asked.

"It sounds like it," Baines said. "And guess what? He's going to get his wish." A wicked smile lit Max Baines's face as he raised his pistol to Joe's head.

In that instant the night lit up. Searchlights played over them, beamed down from a squadron of helicopters that suddenly descended on them. Frank realized that the engine noise from the ship and the barge had masked the rotors' roar until the choppers were right on top of them.

Startled, Max Baines raised his head. Joe reared back and kicked the gun out of the shipowner's hand. Frank rolled quickly, smacking his elbow into a seaman's nose, then sprang to his feet, ready for action.

"Frank!" he heard Joe yell. "Look!"

Frank turned to see the choppers hovering close to the deck and marines hopping down onto the ship, guns at the ready. "Put down your weapons!" ordered a voice over a loudspeaker. "This is the U.S. Marine Corps. You are all under arrest, by order of the U.S. Coast Guard and the FBI!"

It was all over in minutes. To Frank's satisfaction, all hands were soon in custody. "Want a lift back to town?" a helmeted marine captain asked Frank with a grin.

"You bet, sir!" Frank said. "How did you guys reach us so fast?"

"They got the message at the coast guard station while we were on open sea maneuvers about twenty miles from here."

"Good job, soldier," Joe said.

"Thank you, sir." The marine stood aside to let Frank and Joe climb up the ladder to the helicopter first. He saluted the Hardys, and chuckling, the Hardys saluted back.

It was Monday, the day the maritime court inquiry would have taken place, and Frank and Joe were preparing to cast off from San Juan harbor on the *Sun Dancer*.

"Are you sure you don't want to press charges against Vince Brewer?" Lieutenant Lily Brown repeated for the umpteenth time. She was standing on the deck of the sailboat in her crisp white uniform, saying goodbye. Frank admired the way her green eyes and blond hair sparkled in the sunlight.

"We told you," Joe repeated in an exasperated monotone, "we feel sorry for the guy. What he did was wrong, but no one got hurt. He has enough problems without being tried for attempted murder."

"Oh, all right. It's just that if you had to come back and testify, I'd get to see you again."

"Alex Baines has put in a new claim for the insurance money on the freighter, right? Frank and I might have to testify for that," Joe said.

"And what about Max Baines's trial?" Frank added. "We might all be called for that."

"A lot of important people are pretty impressed with you these days," Lily added. "Including the president of a small island nation, the owner of a San Juan shipping company, a ship's captain, and my boss. Major Rivera said to tell you anytime you come back to visit, you have free use of his private fishing boat."

"See? There's a good reason to come back right there." Frank smiled at her.

"Oh! I almost forgot to tell you," Lily said, blushing. "We found the last missing sailor!"

"Wow!" Joe said. "Is he alive?"

"Alive and several thousand dollars richer!" Lily told them. "He washed up on the shore of a resort hotel after just a few hours in the water. He was in such good shape that his credit cards were still in his wallet. He was so glad to be alive that he booked a room in the hotel and stayed for a week. By the time we located him, he'd made a small fortune playing blackjack in the casino. He won every single night!"

"Great." Frank was very pleased. "Happy endings all around—at least for almost everyone."

"And now," Joe said, smiling sadly, "I'll have to ask you to step onto the pier. The *Sun Dancer*'s ready to roll."

"What's the weather forecast, Lieutenant?" Frank asked as he took his place behind the wheel and turned on the small motor.

"Clear skies ahead," Lily replied smartly, stepping onto shore. "See you, guys." She waved as the Hardys maneuvered the yacht out into the harbor. "Don't forget the major's offer, okay?"

Smiling with anticipation, Frank and Joe steered the graceful sloop toward open water, cruising close to a sleek, modern-looking cargo ship. As they passed the bridge, the ship's horn blasted out a greeting. They saw Captain Evans waving down at them, beaming. "Don't worry, boys!" he shouted, cupping his hands to his mouth. "I won't run you down!"

Frank and Joe's next case:

Frank and Joe are learning the true meaning of the words *Wild West*. Invited to stay at a ranch in the Texas Panhandle, they arrive just in time to attend the Dry Valley Rodeo. The star of the show is a rugged young cowboy named Buck—but his day in the sun is about to take a dark turn: he's riding straight into a Texas-size setup!

Buck's high-powered performance is abruptly cut short by a high-powered rifle, and the Hardys are determined to find out why. The truth may lie in Buck's shadowy past or in his sudden success, but one thing's for sure: money and lives are at stake. The boys had better learn the rodeo ropes fast, or they may be the ones to bite the dust . . . in *Rough Riding,* Case #68 in The Hardy Boys Casefiles™.